FREE?

STORIES ABOUT HUMAN RIGHTS

AMNESTY
INTERNATIONAL

CANDLEWICK PRESS

Copyright © 2009 by Amnesty International UK

First U.S. edition 2010

Compilation copyright © 2009 by Amnesty International UK
Foreword copyright © 2009 by Jacqueline Wilson
"Klaus Vogel and the Bad Lads" copyright © 2009 by David Almond
"School Slave" copyright © 2009 by Theresa Breslin
"Scout's Honour" copyright © 2009 by Sarah Mussi
"Sarsaparilla" copyright © 2009 by Ursula Dubosarsky
"After the Hurricane" copyright © 2009 by Rita Williams-Garcia
"If Only Papa Hadn't Danced" copyright © by 2009 Patricia McCormick
"Prince Francis" copyright © 2009 by Roddy Doyle
"Uncle Meena" copyright © 2009 by Ibtisam Barakat
"Searching for a Two-Way Street" copyright © 2009 by Malorie Blackman
"Setting Words Free" copyright © 2009 by Margaret Mahy
"Jojo Learns to Dance" copyright © 2009 by Meja Mwangi
"Wherever I Lay Down My Head" copyright © 2009 by Jamila Gavin
"Christopher" copyright © 2008 by Eoin Colfer
"No Trumpets Needed" copyright © 2007 by Michael Morpurgo

Library of Congress Cataloging-in-Publication Data

Free? : stories about human rights / Amnesty International. — 1st U.S. ed.
p. cm.
Summary: An anthology of fourteen stories by young adult authors from around the world, on such themes as asylum, law, education, and faith, compiled in honor of the sixtieth anniversary of the Universal Declaration of Human Rights.
Contents: Klaus Vogel and the bad lads / by David Almond — School slave / by Theresa Breslin — Scout's honour / by Sarah Mussi — Sarsaparilla / by Ursula Dubosarsky — After the hurricane / by Rita Williams-Garcia — If only Papa hadn't danced / by Patricia McCormick — Prince Francis / by Roddy Doyle — Uncle Meena / by Ibtisam Barakat — Searching for a two-way street / by Malorie Blackman — Setting words free / by Margaret Mahy — Jojo learns to dance / by Meja Mwangi — Wherever I lay down my head / by Jamila Gavin — Christopher / by Eoin Colfer — No trumpets needed / by Michael Morpurgo.

1. Short stories. 2. Human rights — Juvenile fiction. [1. Short stories. 2. Human rights — Fiction. 3. Freedom — Fiction. 4. United Nations. General Assembly. Universal Declaration of Human Rights.] I. Amnesty International. II. Title.
PZ5.F854 2010
[Fic] — dc22   2009014720

ISBN 978-0-7636-4703-2 (hardcover)
ISBN 978-0-7636-4926-5 (paperback)

10 11 12 13 14 15 MVP 10 9 8 7 6 5 4 3 2 1

Printed in York, PA, U.S.A.

This book was typeset in Frutiger Light and Carimbo.

Candlewick Press
99 Dover Street
Somerville, Massachusetts 02144

visit us at www.candlewick.com

CONTENTS

ARTICLE 1
UNIVERSAL DECLARATION
OF HUMAN RIGHTS, 1948

FOREWORD

WE used to have a delightful art teacher at my secondary school, who designed a joke school badge for us—of two demonic schoolgirls fighting with field hockey sticks, with a special school motto underneath: *It's not fair!* He said these were the three words we used most often. We said it wasn't fair we had to wear such a revolting school uniform; it wasn't fair we had so much homework to do; it wasn't fair we had to eat such disgusting school dinners.

I whined as much as anyone—and then when I was twelve, I read *The Diary of a Young Girl* by Anne Frank. I felt so ashamed. Life truly was desperately unfair for Anne, having to hide month after month in the Secret Annexe, in fear of her life. I cried when I reached the end of the book and learnt what had happened to Anne, but although she died tragically young, her wonderful diary is a lasting testament to her life and the persecution of so many Jews during the last world war.

So many brave writers have drawn attention to the horrors of repressive regimes, even though they've suffered as a result. The authors contributing stories to this beautiful book have given us much food for thought. Life *isn't* fair—but we can do our best to right the wrongs.

Let's all join together and live by the thirty rules of the Universal Declaration of Human Rights.

Jacqueline Wilson

KLAUS VOGEL
AND THE BAD LADS

David Almond

WE'D been together for years. We called ourselves the Bad Lads, but it was just a joke. We were mischief-makers, pests, and scamps. We never caused proper trouble — not till that autumn, anyway; round about the time we were turning thirteen; round about the time Klaus Vogel came.

The regulars were me, Tonto McKenna from Stivvey Court, Dan Digby, and the Spark twins, Fred and Frank. We all came from Felling, and we all went to St. John's. Then there was Joe Gillespie. He was a year or so older than the rest of us, and kept himself a bit aloof, but he was the leader, and he was great. His hair was long and curled over his collar. He wore faded Levi's, Chelsea boots, Ben Sherman shirts. He had a girlfriend, Teresa Doyle. He used to walk hand in hand with her through Holly Hill Park.

I used to dream about being just like Joe — flicking my hair back with my hand, winking at girls, putting my arm round one of the lads after a specially good stunt, saying, "We done really good, didn't we? We're really bad, aren't we? Ha ha ha!"

All of us, not just me, wanted to be a bit like Joe in those days.

Most days after school, we took a ball onto the playing field at Swards Road and put two jumpers down for a goal. We played keep-up and penalties, practised diving headers, swerves, and traps. We played matches with tiny teams and a single goal, but we still got carried away by it all, just like when we were eight or nine. We called each other Bestie, Pele, Yashin, and commentated on the moves: "He's beaten one man; he's beaten two! Can he do it? *Yeees!* Oh, no! Oh, what a save by the black-clad Russian!" We punched the air when we scored a goal and waved at the invisible roaring crowd. Our voices echoed across the playing field and over the rooftops. Our breath rose in plumes as the air chilled and the evening came on.

We felt ecstatic, transfigured. Then, after a while, one of us would see Joe coming out from among the houses, and we'd come back down to the real world.

Joe usually had a trick or two of his own lined up, but he

always made a point of asking what we fancied doing next.

Tonto might say, "We could play knocky nine door in Balaclava Street."

Or Frank might go, "Jump through the hedges in Coldwell Park Drive?"

But we'd all just groan at things like that. They were little kids' tricks, and we'd done them tons of times before. Sometimes there were new ideas, like the night we howled like ghosts through Mrs. Minto's letter box, or when we phoned the police and said an escaped lunatic was chopping up Miss O'Sullivan in her front garden, or when we tied a length of string at head height right across Dunelm Terrace. But usually the best plans turned out to be Joe's. It was his idea, for instance, to put the broken bottles under Mr. Tatlock's car tyres, and to dig up the leeks in Albert Finch's allotment. We went along with Joe, but by the time that autumn came, some of his plans were starting to trouble us all.

One evening, when the sky was glowing red over St. Patrick's steeple, and when it was obvious that none of us had anything new to suggest, Joe rubbed his hands together and grinned. He had a rolled-up newspaper stuck into his jeans pocket.

"It's a cold night, lads," he said. "How about a bit of a blaze to warm us up?"

"A blaze?" said Tonto.

"Aye." Joe winked. He rattled a box of matches. "Follow me."

He led us up Swards Road and across The Drive and into the narrow lane behind Sycamore Grove. We stopped in the near darkness under a great overgrown privet hedge. Joe told us to be quiet and to gather close.

"Just look at the state of this," he whispered.

He put his hand up into the foliage and shook it. Dust and litter and old dead leaves fell out of it. I scratched at something crawling in my hair.

"Would *your* dads let *your* hedge get into a mess like this?" he said.

"No," we answered.

"No. It's just like he is. Crazy and stupid and wild."

"Like who?" whispered Frank.

"Like him inside!" said Joe. "Like Useless Eustace!"

Mr. Eustace. He lived in the house beyond the hedge. No family, hardly any pals. He'd been a teacher for a while, but he'd given up. Now he spent most of his time stuck inside writing poems, reading books, listening to weird music.

"We're gonna burn it down," said Joe.

"Eh?" I said.

"The hedge. Burn it down, teach him a lesson."

The hedge loomed above us against the darkening sky.

4

"Why?"

Joe sighed. "Cos it's a mess and cos we're the Bad Lads. And he deserves it."

He unrolled the newspaper and started shoving pages into the hedge. He handed pages to us as well. "Stuff them low down," he said, "so it'll catch better."

I held back. I imagined the roar of the flames, the belching smoke. "I don't think we should," I found myself saying.

The other lads watched as Joe grabbed my collar and glared into my eyes.

"You think too much," he whispered. "You're a Bad Lad. So *be* a Bad Lad."

He finished shoving the paper in. He got the matches out. "Anyway," he said, "he was a bloody conchie, wasn't he?"

"That was ages back. He was only doing what he believed in."

"He was a coward and a conchie. And like me dad says—once a conchie . . ."

"Don't do it, Joe."

"You gonna be a conchie, too?" he said. "*Are* you?" He looked at all of us. "Are *any* of you going to be conchies?"

"No," we said.

"Good lads." He put his arm round my shoulder.

"Blame me," he whispered. "I'm the leader. You're only following instructions. So do it."

I hated myself, but I shoved my bit of crumpled paper into the hedge with the rest of them.

Conchie. The story came from before any of us were born. Mr. Eustace wouldn't fight in the Second World War. He was against all war; he couldn't attack his fellow man. He was a conscientious objector. When my dad and the other lads' dads went off to risk their lives fighting the Germans and the Japanese, Mr. Eustace was sent to jail, then let out to work on a farm in Durham.

He'd suffered then; he'd suffered since. My dad said he'd been a decent bloke, but turning conchie had ruined his life. He'd never find peace. He should have left this place and started a new life somewhere else, but he never did.

Joe lit a match and held it to the paper. Flames flickered. They started rising fast. Tonto was already backing away down the lane; Fred and Frank were giggling; Dan had disappeared. I cursed. For a moment, I couldn't move. Then we were all away, running hunched over through the shadows, and the hedge was roaring behind us. By the time we were back at Swards Road, there was a great orange glow over Sycamore Grove, and smoke was belching up towards the stars.

"Now that," said Joe, "is what I call a proper Bad Lads stunt!"

And no matter what we thought inside, all of us shivered with the thrill of it.

Next morning I went back to the lane. It was black and soaking wet from the ash and the hosepipes. The hedge was just a few black twisted stems. Mr. Eustace was in the garden talking to a policeman. He kept shrugging, shaking his head. He caught my eye and I wanted to yell out, "You're useless! What did you expect? You should have started a new life somewhere else!"

Joe was nowhere in sight, but Fred and Frank were grinning from further down the lane. Neighbours were out, muttering and whispering. None of them suspected anything, of course. They knew us. We were Felling lads. There was no badness in us. Not really.

That was the week Klaus Vogel arrived. He was a scrawny little kid from East Germany. The tale was that his dad was a famous singer who'd been hauled off to a prison camp somewhere in Russia. The mother had disappeared—shot, more than likely, people said. The kid had been smuggled out in the boot of a car. Nobody knew the full truth, said my dad, not when it had happened so far away and in countries like that. Just be happy we lived in a place like this, where we could go about as we pleased.

Klaus stayed in the priest's house next to St. Patrick's

and joined our school, St. John's. He didn't have a word of English, but he was bright and he learnt fast. Within a few days he could speak a few English words in a weird Geordie–German accent. Soon he was even writing a few words in English.

We looked at his book one break.

"How the hell do you *do* it?" asked Dan.

Klaus raised his hands. He didn't know how to explain. "I just . . ." he began, and he scribbled hard and fast. "Like so," he said.

We saw jagged English words mingled with what had to be German.

"What is it?" said Tonto.

"Is story of my *Vater*. My father. It must be . . ." Klaus frowned into the air, seeking the word.

"Must be *told*," I said.

"*Danke*. Thank you." He nodded and his eyes widened. "It must be told. *Ja!* Aye!"

And we all laughed at the way he used the Tyneside word.

After school Klaus talked with his feet. Overhead kicks, sudden body swerves, curling free kicks: the kind of football we could only dream of. He was tiny, clever, tough. We gasped in admiration. When he played, he lost himself in the game, and all his troubles seemed to fall away.

"What'll we call you?" asked Frank.

Klaus frowned. "Klaus Vogel," he said.

"No. Your football name. I'm Pele. You are . . ."

Klaus pondered. He glanced around, as if to check who was listening. "Müller," he murmured. "*Ja!* Gerd Müller!"

Then he grinned, twisted, dodged a tackle, swerved the ball into the corner of the invisible net, and waved to the invisible crowd. All the lads yelled, "Yeah! Well done, Müller!"

The first time Klaus Vogel met Joe was a few weeks after he'd arrived. Since the hedge-burning, things had gone quiet. Joe spent most of his time with Teresa Doyle. We'd seen him a couple of times, leaning against a fence on Swards Road watching us play, but he hadn't come across. Now here he was, strolling onto the field in the icy November dusk. I moved to Klaus's side.

"He's called Joe," I whispered. "He's OK."

"So this is the famous Klaus Vogel," said Joe.

Klaus shrugged. Joe smiled.

"And your dad's the famous singer, eh? The *op-era* singer."

"Aye."

"Giz a song, then."

"What?" said Klaus.

"He must've taught you, eh? And we like a bit of *op-era*

here, don't we, lads? Go on, giz a song." Joe demonstrated. He opened his mouth wide and stretched his hand out like he was singing to an audience. "Go on. You're in a free country now, you know. Sing up!"

Klaus stared at him. I wanted to say, "Don't do it," but Klaus had stepped away, closer to Joe. He took a deep breath and started to sing. His voice rang out across the field. It was weird, like the music that drifted from Mr. Eustace's house. We heard the loveliness in it. How could he *do* such things?

But Joe was bent over, struggling with laughter, and then he was waving his hands to bring Klaus to a halt.

Klaus stopped, stared again. "You do not like?" he asked.

Joe wiped the tears of laughter from his eyes. "Aye, aye," he said. "It's brilliant, son."

Then Joe opened his own mouth and started singing, a wobbly high-pitched imitation of Klaus. He looked at us, and we all started to laugh with him.

"Mebbe we're just not ready for it, eh, lads?"

"Mebbe we're not," muttered Frank, turning his eyes away.

Klaus looked at us, too. Then he just shrugged again. "So. I will go home," he said.

"No," said Joe. "You can't."

"Can't?"

"We can't let you." He grinned. He winked. "We got to initiate him, haven't we, lads? We got to make him one of the Bad Lads." He showed his teeth like he was a great beast, then he smiled. "Specially when you consider where he comes from, eh?"

"What you mean?" asked Klaus.

"From *Germany*," said Joe. "Not so long ago we'd have been wanting to kill you. You'd've been wanting to kill us."

He raised his hand like he had a gun in it and pointed it at Klaus. He pulled an imaginary trigger. Then he smiled. "It's nowt, son," he said. "Just some carry-on. What'll it be, lads? Knocky nine door in Balaclava Street? Jumping through hedges in Coldwell Park Drive?"

"The hedges," I said. I put my hand on Klaus's shoulder. "It's OK," I whispered. "We're just messing about. And it's on your way home."

So Klaus came with us. We cut through the lanes to Coldwell Park Drive and slipped into the gardens behind, then Joe led us and we charged over the back lawns and through the hedges while dogs howled and people yelled at us to cut it out. We streamed out, giggling, onto Felling Bank. Joe held us in a quick huddle and said it was just like the old days. He put his arm round Klaus.

"Ha!" he said. "You're a proper Bad Lad now, Herr Vogel. You're one of us!"

Then we started running our separate ways through the shadows.

Klaus caught my arm. "Why?" he said.

"Why what?"

"Why we do *that*? Why we do what Joe says?"

"It's not like that," I said. I paused. "It's . . ." But my voice felt all caught up inside me, like it couldn't find words.

"Is *what*?" said Klaus.

He held me like he really wanted to understand. But I had no answers. Klaus shrugged his shoulders, shook his head, walked away.

Klaus kept away from the Bad Lads for a while. He scribbled in his book, writing his story. He sang out loud in music lessons. He dazzled everyone with his football skills during games. There were rumours that the body of his mother had turned up. The whole school prayed for the liberation of East Germany, for the conversion of Russia, for Klaus Vogel and his family.

One day after school, I came upon him walking under the trees on Watermill Lane. He walked quickly, swinging his arms, singing softly.

"Klaus!" I said. "What you doing?"

"I am being free!" he said. "My father said that one day I would walk as a free man. I would walk and sing and show the world that I am free. So I do it. Look!"

He strode in circles, swinging his arms again.

"Do I look like I am free?" he said.

"Yes." I laughed. "Of course you do."

He laughed, too. "Ha! As I walk I think of him in his cell. I think of her."

"They would be proud of you," I said.

"Would they?"

"Yes."

He laughed again, a bitter laugh. "And as I walk I think of my friends here," he said. "I think of you; I think of Joe."

"Of Joe?"

"*Ja!* Him!"

"You think too much, Klaus. Come and play football, will you? Come and be Gerd Müller."

And he sighed and shrugged. "OK."

It was getting dark. Frost already glistened on the field. The stars were like a field of vivid frost above. Klaus played with more brilliance and passion than ever. We watched him in wonder. He ran with the ball at his feet; he flicked it into the goal; he leapt with joy; he danced to the crowd.

Then Joe was there, his footsteps crackling across the grass. He had a small rucksack on his back.

"Herr Vogel," he said. "Nice to see you again."

He stepped closer and put his arm round Klaus's

shoulders. "Sorry to hear about . . ." He held up his hand, as if to restrain his own words. "Our thoughts are with you, son."

He turned to the rest of us. "Now, lads. It's a fine night for a Bad Lads stunt."

You could tell it was almost over with us and Joe. We gathered around him reluctantly; our smiles were forced when he told us he had the perfect trick. But he was tall and strong. He smelt of aftershave; he wore a black Ben Sherman, black jeans, black Chelsea boots. We hadn't broken free of him. He drew us into a huddle. He smiled and told us we'd always been the Bad Lads and we'd keep on being the Bad Lads, wouldn't we?

No one said no. No one objected when he told us to follow. I think I hesitated for a moment, but Klaus came to my side and whispered, "You will not go? But you must. We must all follow our leader, mustn't we?"

And Klaus stepped ahead, and I followed.

Joe led us to The Drive, towards the lane behind Sycamore Grove.

"Not again." I sighed.

"It's like me dad says," said Joe. "He should've been drove out years back." He turned to Klaus. "It's local stuff, son. Probably your lot had better ways of dealing with the Eustaces than we ever had."

Klaus just shrugged.

"Anyway, lads. It's just a bit of fun this time." He opened his rucksack, took out a box of eggs. "Here, one each. Hit a window for a hundred points."

A couple of the lads giggled. They took their eggs. Joe held the box out to me. I hesitated. Klaus took one and looked at me. So I took an egg and held it in my hand.

Joe smiled and patted Klaus's shoulder. "Good Bad Lad, Herr Vogel," he murmured.

Klaus laughed his bitter laugh again. *"Nein,"* he said. "I am not a good Bad Lad. I am Klaus Vogel."

He stepped towards Joe.

"No, Klaus," I muttered. I tried to hold him back, but he stepped right up to Joe.

"I do not like you," he said. "I do not like the things you make others do."

"Oh! You *do not like*?" said Joe.

"Nein."

Joe laughed. He mocked the word—*"Nein! Nein! Nein!"*—as he stamped the earth and gave a Nazi salute. He grabbed Klaus by the collar, but Klaus didn't recoil.

"You could crush me in a moment," he said. "But I am not . . . *ängstlich*."

"Frightened," I said.

"*Ja!* I am not frightened. *Ich bin frei!*"

"Ha! *Frei. Frei.*"

"He is free," I said. And in that moment, I knew that

he *was* free, despite his father's imprisonment, despite his mother's death, despite Joe's fist gripping his collar. He had said no. He was free.

Joe snarled and drew his fist back. I found myself reaching out. I caught the fist in midair.

"No," I said. "You can't do that."

"What?"

"I said no!"

Joe thumped us both that night, in the lane behind Mr. Eustace's house. We fought back, but he was tall and strong and there was little we could do against his savagery. Tonto and the others had disappeared. Afterwards I walked home with Klaus through the frosty starlit night. We were sore and we had blood on our faces, but soon we were swinging our arms.

"Do I look like I am free?" I said.

Klaus laughed. "*Ja!* Yes! Aye!"

And he began to sing, and I tried to join in.

A couple of days later he came with me to Mr. Eustace's house. I knocked at the door, and Mr. Eustace opened it.

"I burned down your hedge," I said.

He peered at me. "Did you, now?" he said.

I chewed my lips. Music was playing. Beyond Mr. Eustace the hallway was lined with books.

"I'm sorry," I said. "I was wrong."

"Yes, you were."

I felt so clumsy, so stupid.

"This is Klaus Vogel," I said. "He is a writer, a footballer, a singer."

"Then he is a civilized man. Perhaps you can learn from him."

I nodded. I was about to turn and lead Klaus away, but Mr. Eustace said, "Why don't you come inside?"

We followed him in. There were books everywhere. In the living room was an open notebook on a desk with an uncapped fountain pen lying upon it. The writing in the book was in the shape of poetry.

Mr. Eustace stood at the window and indicated the ruined hedge outside. "Is that how you wish the world to be?" he asked me.

"No," I answered.

"No."

He made us tea. There were fig rolls and little cakes. He spoke a few words to Klaus in German, and Klaus gasped with pleasure. Then Mr. Eustace put another record on. Opera. High, sweet voices flowing together and filling the house with their sound.

"Mozart!" said Klaus.

"Yes."

Klaus joined in. His voice rang out. Mr. Eustace closed his eyes and smiled.

ARTICLE 1

WE ARE ALL BORN FREE AND EQUAL. WE ALL HAVE
OUR OWN THOUGHTS AND IDEAS. WE SHOULD ALL
BE TREATED IN THE SAME WAY.

SCHOOL SLAVE

Theresa Breslin

MONDAY was never a good day in school for Ryan.

Monday was the day the class assistant took him for extra work. Maths before break; English after lunch. He didn't like either. Numbers did his head in; words made his eyes ache.

Ryan squinted in the morning sunlight. Took in the trees by the canal, the bushes at the water's edge. All just beginning to bud. This time of the year was fascinating, with the migrating birds returning, and Ryan loved to dawdle along, often losing all sense of time. There was a huge swans' nest beside the towpath here. Last spring he'd been late for school on at least half a dozen occasions because he'd stopped so often to watch the elegant birds building it. Maybe they'd come back and use it again this spring. He'd rather stay here and watch for the swans' arrival than go to school and do rubbish maths and English.

He really resented it. Being made to do work he didn't want to do. In school. Every day. A slave, that's what he was.

Ryan kicked a stone from the path. It shot through the air and hit the water with a splash. The ripples surged in a wide circle and wobbled a plastic takeaway container that had been drifting along midstream. It almost overturned. He hated people chucking plastic stuff in the water. Once he'd found a heron lying dead among the reeds, choked on a carrier bag.

Ryan lifted a bigger stone and lobbed it at the carton, trying to sink it. The stone missed its target but caused enough movement to send the carton spinning towards the bank. He grabbed a stick, hooked the box, and picked it up. Inside was a scrap of red cloth. On it, someone had scrawled one word:

HELP

Ryan stared at it in surprise. He took the cloth and smoothed it out. There was no other mark on it. Just the one word in thick brown lettering:

HELP

Someone playing a joke, surely. Ryan scrunched it up and shoved it in his pocket. He'd show it to his classmates, and they'd have a good laugh making up stupid reasons for how it had got there. He glanced at his watch. He'd better hurry or he'd be late for school again. His mum would have a fit if he got any more detentions.

But, slaving away all day in school, Ryan forgot about the message in the takeaway carton. It wasn't until he was by the canal on his way home that he remembered. He pulled the scrap of red cloth from his pocket to look at it again.

The word had almost disappeared. Most of the brown lettering had become powdery and had flaked off. Ryan touched it with his finger and realized it was dried-out mud. It was as if the person who had written it had dipped their own finger in mud to write the message. Who would do a crazy thing like that?

Ryan knew this part of the canal really well. Most days he walked back and forth to school this way. At the moment, there were no muddy stretches. The weather had been dry for days. But the writing had been quite fresh when he'd seen it this morning. Where could the box have come from?

Ryan frowned. The canal wasn't exactly a river, but the water did flow along in a dreamy sort of a manner. The takeaway carton had been drifting downstream, so it must have been put in the water somewhere higher up, beyond Ryan's house. And then he recalled a cutting just past the end of the town—a loop of water running off to one side past a derelict boatyard. There would be mud there, he thought. Wet mud.

He checked the time on his phone and then texted his mum: *B a bit L8.* It would take him just over five minutes to run there, and then a few more to have a quick look around. He would be home about fifteen minutes later than usual. She wouldn't worry about fifteen minutes.

Ryan raced along the canal toward the old boatyard. Here the towpath swung away from the water and up to the main road. Far down below, on the entrance gate to the disused yard, was a sign showing a skull and cross-bones and a warning to keep out. But nobody could get in anyway. At the foot of the incline was a high, sturdy fence with vicious barbed wire coiled at the top. Inside the perimeter, thick tangles of nettles and thorn bushes grew. You could hardly glimpse the broken-down building of the old boathouse with its boarded-up windows.

Ryan slid down the slope and explored the whole length of the fence. There was no way in. Nobody about and nothing to see. Yet . . . something was not quite right. What was it? His teachers were always telling him off for not concentrating in class, but he didn't mind trying to fig- ure out this kind of problem. Ryan thought hard, trying to work out what was wrong. Everything was quiet. He studied the boathouse more closely. And then he realized what the silence meant. No birds! It was the perfect place for nesting birds, yet there were none fluttering around the low rooftop. Why not?

Ryan's phone bleeped. It was his mum replying to his text.

Why will U B L8? What have U been up 2?

Ryan grimaced. She knew how much he hated school and how often he got into trouble for not doing his work properly. She would think he was in detention. He replied by punching in a zero. His thumb was about to hit *send,* when he was suddenly aware of movement from the other side of the barbed-wire fence. He lifted his head. A long scarf was being pushed through a gap in one of the boarded-up windows.

It was bright red.

Ryan's heart began to beat faster. He gripped the scrap of red material in his pocket. It had to be the same person who had written the message! They were trying to attract his attention!

But why? Was a kidnap victim being held inside the boathouse? Not very likely. Nothing exciting ever happened in this town. There was no point in him calling the police, Ryan decided. At the sound of his voice they'd know right off that he was young, and they'd probably think it was a hoax. He'd heard a story about some teenagers using their mobiles to report a car accident and no one believing them. And in any case it might be somebody mucking about inside the old boatyard, having a big laugh at his expense. The police would trace the call to his mobile and he'd have it taken off him for making nuisance calls.

Yet he couldn't just walk away, could he? Not without being sure.

Ryan looked at the phone in his hand. If he was going to try to get inside the yard to find out what was going on, it would take him more than fifteen minutes. He'd need to tell his mum something to give himself enough time to investigate properly.

His phone bleeped again.

Have U got detention?

His mum had thought of the perfect excuse for him! Ryan punched out his reply.

Yes. I'll B home in 1hr.

He waited. Knowing what was coming next. Sure enough, within seconds his phone bleeped.

U R grounded!

Ryan shoved his phone into his pocket.

The first problem to figure out was how to get past the barbed wire. The fence ran all the way around the boathouse and went right down to the old stone quay on each side. Ryan went to the water's edge, hunkered down on the canal bank, and peered carefully round the fence. He drew in his breath. Below him a narrow ledge ran along the side of the quay, wide enough for one person to walk on.

It led to the door of the boathouse, which opened directly onto the water of the inlet.

Ryan dumped his school bag on the bank and lowered himself onto the ledge. He inched forward until he came to the boathouse door. It was secured by a long metal bolt and a heavy padlock.

The padlock was new.

Locked from the *outside.*

If there was anyone in there, then they were a prisoner. Maybe not an *actual* prisoner, but definitely trapped inside.

A jumble of thoughts went through Ryan's mind. Perhaps someone had been playing on the roof and it had collapsed and they'd crashed to the ground and injured themselves so they couldn't climb back out and they didn't have a mobile phone. That was it! And no one could hear their cries for help because the boathouse was so far from the towpath.

Ryan examined the door. It had a gap at the bottom. Wide enough for a person to push a takeaway carton into the water and propel it towards the canal. He put his ear against the wood.

Silence.

"Hello?" he called out.

There was a scuttling sound. The thought of rats entered Ryan's head. Enormous rats. With sharp teeth. Then he remembered the red scarf. He hadn't come this far only to go home without finding out who had asked for help.

He forced a passage through the overgrown bushes round the side of the building to where he'd seen the red scarf fluttering through the gap in the boarded-up window. The scarf had gone, but the gap was wide enough for him to see through.

Ryan put his eye to the gap.

Another eye looked out at him.

Ryan cried out and jumped backwards. At the same moment, from the other side of the wooden boarding, he heard a girl scream.

"Sorry," Ryan called out when he had recovered. "Sorry," he said again, and when there was no reply, he added, "I found your message asking for help. I saw your red scarf at the window."

"You, the boy I see?" The voice was hardly above a whisper.

"That's me," said Ryan. "Who are you?"

"You, the boy? Yes?" It was a girl's voice, sounding very scared. A girl who didn't speak English very well.

"I'm the boy," Ryan replied. "How did you get trapped in there?"

"I want go out. I want go out."

"OK. OK." Ryan looked around. He lifted a stout stick and pushed it through the gap. "Stand to one side," he ordered. Then he levered the stick against the panelling until the wood split and the gap was bigger. Bracing one foot against the wall, he grasped the edges of the board and hauled with all his strength. With a wrenching, tearing noise, a section broke off.

A young girl about ten years old stood in front of him.

"Come on," Ryan said. "I'll help you climb out."

She looked at him for a moment and then spoke slowly. "And the others."

Ryan stared at her. "What others?"

"The others."

"There are other people in there with you?"

The girl nodded.

"Then why didn't you all break down this boarding yourselves?"

The girl didn't speak, only gazed at Ryan as though she didn't fully trust him.

Ryan made beckoning motions. "Come out," he urged. "Everyone come out."

The girl shook her head and beckoned in turn to Ryan. "Come in," she said. "Help. Children." She made a sign with her hand to indicate someone smaller than she was.

"You mean *little* children?" Ryan asked in astonishment.

The girl nodded.

Ryan hesitated. Something was going on here that he

didn't understand, and it was beginning to make him very uneasy.

Suddenly, both of them heard a noise. It came from beyond the towpath, near the main road.

The sound of a van door banging shut.

The girl put her hand to her mouth and gave a moan. It was more than fear. Real terror showed on her face.

"Go," she said urgently to Ryan. "He hurt you."

Ryan glanced behind and above him. But the main road couldn't be seen from here. "Who?"

"Bad man." The girl flapped her hand at Ryan in agitation. "Go! Go!" And she ran off into the darkness of the building.

Ryan pulled out his mobile. He definitely had to call the police now. But the problem was still the same. What if they didn't believe him? And if he called his mum, it would take too long to explain it all. By the time she'd stopped shrieking at him for lying about being in detention, it would be too late. The man, whoever he was, would have arrived at the boathouse. Ryan knew he needed do something. Something quite drastic.

With shaking fingers he punched out a text to his mum and pressed *send*. Then, quite deliberately, he switched off his mobile.

It should be easy enough to hide in the nearby bushes, he thought. Then he remembered his school bag, left lying on the bank beside the fence. The man would see it when he reached the canal!

As fast as he dared, Ryan scurried back along the ledge of the quay. He grabbed his bag and dived behind a tree just as a man came clambering down from the towpath. Ryan held his breath as the man passed within a metre of where he was hidden. He tensed himself to run, and then a thought struck him.

When the man opened the boathouse door, he would see at once that someone had been there. He would notice the panelling ripped from one of the windows. What would he do to the girl when he saw this? Almost certainly he'd take her and whoever else was inside away in his van before help arrived. Or he might do something worse.

Ryan shivered.

"Excuse me!"

"What?" The man turned. He'd been about to crouch down to climb onto the stone ledge.

"Excuse me." Ryan was so scared, his voice sounded shrill.

"What do you want?" the man demanded. "What are you doing here?"

Ryan said the first thing that came into his head. "Looking for swans."

"Swans?" the man repeated.

"Yes," said Ryan, thinking frantically. He tried to do a

quick sum in his head. If help was coming at all, it would be from the other end of town. There were three sets of traffic lights between there and here. Supposing they were all on red? A minute's wait at each light plus a minute's travel time between each one. Three times two equalled six. That meant at least six minutes before he could expect anyone to arrive. *Six minutes.* He had to keep this man talking for six minutes.

"No swans here," the man said firmly. "Try further on."

Ryan attempted a smile. He unhitched the fastening of his school bag and drew out a notebook. "I'm on a nature study thing, er, and so—"

"Clear off," the man said abruptly.

"But I really need to do this homework," Ryan protested nervously.

"Go away, *now!*" He made a move towards Ryan, who stumbled back. The man raised his hand, and then stopped, listening.

Piercing the air, rising and falling like a demented banshee, came the very distinct wail of a fire engine.

Ryan could have cried in relief.

"*Less* than six minutes," he said aloud. "I forgot—fire engines are allowed to crash red lights."

And then he saw his mum running, half falling, down the slope.

"Ryan, Ryan!" she was yelling at the top of her voice.

"Are you all right? Where's the fire?"

The man looked at Ryan. "Fire?"

"There's no fire," Ryan admitted.

"No fire," the man repeated.

Ryan's mum turned on him in fury. "You texted me to call the fire brigade because the old boathouse was on fire with someone trapped inside!"

The man looked from Ryan to the boathouse and back again. Then he hurriedly began to mount the slope towards the main road. But his path was blocked by a fire chief, who was striding down towards Ryan and his mum. The man ducked round him to run away, but he was stopped by a whole group of firemen following close behind. One of them took the man firmly by the arm while the rest rushed towards the boatyard entrance.

"There isn't a fire," Ryan began.

"There isn't a fire?" The fire chief glowered at Ryan. "Calling out the fire service on a false alarm is a very serious offence."

"But—" said Ryan.

His mum shook his shoulder. "I thought you were inside a burning building!" she sobbed. "I thought you needed rescuing."

"Not me, Mum," said Ryan, pointing. "Them."

The other firemen had smashed open the gate to the boatyard and, using their axes, were now hacking at the nearest boarded-up window. A group of small children stood huddled inside.

"It appears that these kiddies were being used as slave workers," the fire chief told Ryan and his mum a short while later. "The inside of the building has been set up as a clothes sweatshop. It's disgusting that children can be exploited like this."

Ryan had explained how he came to be there while he and his mum waited for the police, paramedics, and a child protection officer to arrive. Now the children were being carried out of the boathouse, wrapped up in blankets.

The child protection officer came over to speak to them. She thanked Ryan for the call. "The police will investigate exactly what the situation is in this instance," she said. "It's sometimes the case that their parents are refugees in debt to a ruthless gang leader who demands that they hand over their children to work as unpaid labour."

Ryan stepped aside to allow a fireman carrying a small figure to walk past. "Some of them are *tiny,*" he said.

"No more than toddlers," his mum agreed. "How can anyone treat children so cruelly?"

"It can be big business," the child protection officer replied. "Organized criminals buy children in Third World countries, promising their parents that they'll get an education and employment. Some are trafficked into the UK and kept hidden in out-of-the-way places so no one will find them. But because of Ryan's actions, at least these lucky few might be able to lead a normal life and be educated."

"I'm so proud of him," said Ryan's mum. "No, really, I *am* very proud of you, Ryan. My daydreaming boy switched his mind into gear and worked out the best way of getting help quickly." She grinned at him. "And just think, Ryan, you can boast about this to your teachers and friends. About how you rescued a group of children so that they can attend school every day."

Ryan laughed. "I will," he said. "I will."

And he meant it.

ARTICLE 4
NOBODY HAS ANY RIGHT TO MAKE US A SLAVE. WE CANNOT MAKE ANYONE ELSE OUR SLAVE.

ARTICLE 26
WE ALL HAVE THE RIGHT TO AN EDUCATION.

SCOUT'S HONOUR

Sarah Mussi

CROWN PROSECUTION SERVICE

R. v. Prometheus Prempeh

INDICTMENT

IN THE CROWN COURT AT INNER LONDON,
THE QUEEN v. PROMETHEUS PREMPEH,
PROMETHEUS PREMPEH is charged as follows:

STATEMENT OF OFFENCE

BURGLARY, CONTRARY TO section 9(1)(b) of the Theft Act 1968

PARTICULARS OF OFFENCE

PROMETHEUS PREMPEH on the seventeenth day of January 2009,
having entered as a trespasser a building, namely THE TOWER OF
LONDON, attempted to steal therein THE CROWN JEWELS

Officer of the Court

URN: 09 MM 4536 05

Record of Tape-Recorded Interview

Person interviewed: Prometheus Prempeh
                             (Police exhibit no.:
                             UY/3T)

Age of interviewee: 11 years 2 months

Nationality: Ghanaian

Place of interview: Div. 7 Police Station

No. of pages: 11

Date of interview: 17 January 2009

Time commenced: 18.34

Signature of interviewing senior officer:

C. B. Harrison

Interviewing officer(s): Detective Constable
                            Harrison
                            Police Constable
                            Jenkins

Other persons present: Ms. Flinn
                            (social worker)

INTRODUCTIONS. CAUTION GIVEN TO INTERVIEWEE; FULLY EXPLAINED AND UNDERSTOOD.

Person speaking	_Text_
DC HARRISON	A record is being made of this interview and can be played later. Whatever you say will be transcribed as future evidence. Do you understand that?
PREMPEH	Yes, sir.
DC HARRISON	Can you please explain how you came to be wearing Her Majesty's Crown Jewels at the time of your arrest?
PREMPEH	Yes, sir.
DC HARRISON	Well, please proceed.
PREMPEH	Well, sir, you see, sir, we're on a jamboree visit—I mean, the Kumasi Boy Scouts of Ghana Patrol Division 5, Brong Ahafo Region, are on a world jamboree to London. It's my first time, sir, in England, and I'm very excited and pleased to be here. And I've been doing good too, sir. I've done one good deed every day—and

we went on this outing to the Tower of London, sir, because it was like a treat and we're supposed to have a treat if we're good, sir, and you see, I was playing with my marbles, sir, and our Scout leader, Mr. Acheampong, said I wasn't to play marbles when we were out on Scout business, because you see, sir, Scouts don't do that. Although I don't really know why they don't—if you see what I mean.

DC HARRISON   No, I don't see what you mean—but this is not relevant. Could you acquaint me with how you gained access to the Jewel House?

PREMPEH   Well, please don't tell Mr. Acheampong, will you? But you see, sir, I *was* playing with my marbles and I didn't want to get caught. Because if Mr. Acheampong caught me, that would be the ninth time, and he said if I got caught ten times, he'd take my marbles off me for the rest of the trip. The other boys laugh at me, sir, but they don't realize how much you can do with a marble. And I haven't

	been a Scout for very long, sir, only since I turned eleven, and I want to get my first badge—that's my Accident Prevention Public Service badge, sir—and if he knows . . .
DC HARRISON	I'm not interested in your marbles, or your badge. Can you please respond to the question?
PREMPEH	Am I in a lot of trouble, sir? I didn't mean to do anything. I don't want to be a disgrace to the memory of Lord Robert Baden-Powell. He started the Scouts, sir, and also he's a lord, and he came to Ghana, you know.
DC HARRISON	I didn't.
PREMPEH	He did, sir, and he had a big army and he attacked Kumasi a long time ago, like hundreds of years ago. I expect the people of Kumasi had been bad and that was why Lord Baden-Powell had to attack them—
DC HARRISON	Irrelevant. Can you please continue with your account of the incident for which you were arrested.
PREMPEH	So you see, sir, my best marble—I call it RollerBoy—rolled off the side

of the path and I tried to reach it, but Mr. Acheampong was looking, so I couldn't. And it rolled right down under a big wooden door, and I got really worried, because you see, sir, RollerBoy is my best marble and I won it off Kwaku. He's my friend who likes playing marbles too, sir. He's collecting all the Pokémon ones and he keeps trying to win it back.

DC HARRISON	Get on with the issue in question!
MS. FLINN	Gently, please. The child is only eleven and in a strange country.
PREMPEH	So when Mr. Acheampong had gone on ahead, I ran back and pushed the door. It opened a bit. Then one of those eagles started flapping at me.
PC JENKINS	Ravens.
PREMPEH	I was scared, sir. Anyway, I went in to get RollerBoy, and I tried to keep that eagle out—so I closed the door, you see, and it clicked shut. It locked and I couldn't open it. And I was stuck inside. It was a bit scary, until I found the light switch. And then it wasn't so scary, because I could see it was

a cleaners' cupboard, because there were lots of brooms and things. And I found RollerBoy and I lined him up with HeartofFire—that's my second-best marble—and I couldn't call Mr. Acheampong, because I don't have a British chip in my phone. But I guessed he would notice I wasn't there and come and let me out, but I was a bit worried, because it was nearly closing time at the Palace—Tower.

PC JENKINS
DC HARRISON   Get. On. With. The. Statement.
PREMPEH   Well, I hoped Mr. Acheampong *would* notice before he got back to our hotel, because otherwise he was going to be pretty mad, and all the other boys would be rolling their eyes and saying "Trust Prommy!" And I couldn't tell him about RollerBoy, could I? And I would have to do an awful lot of good deeds to make up for it, and I was a bit worried, really . . .

DC HARRISON   Pause the tape while I go out and *scream.*

MS. FLINN   He's just a child.

40

DC HARRISON	I've got Special Branch, who want *answers*; national security has been *compromised*. The entire street is crowded with *paparazzi*, and all the kid can talk about is losing his *marbles*!
MS. FLINN	Well, that's no excuse for losing yours.
PREMPEH	I did try to remember what we'd learnt in tracking and knotting and signalling, and I tapped out the Morse code SOS, and I was pretty pleased with myself because *O* is one of the hardest for me to remember. But nobody came for ages, and actually I think after *O*, probably *F* is hardest.
PC JENKINS	Who let you out, sonny?
PREMPEH	Uncle Winston—Mr. Owusu—let me out, sir. I discovered he was one of my countrymen from Ghana. He's from Ejisu just like me, and he's one of the security men at the Tower, I think, sir, and I didn't mean to knock him out, and I hope his head gets better, because Lord Baden-Powell

says that all Scouts should know how to do first aid, but I don't. I'm not going on the first-aiders' course until half-term, after I've got my Accident Prevention badge, sir, so I didn't know what to do. I expect Lord Baden-Powell was pretty strict about first aid because so many people died when he attacked Kumasi, and maybe they died because the Ashanti didn't know how to do first aid.

DC HARRISON   Right, Prometheus—

PREMPEH   Prommy, sir, that's what they call me. Prometheus is my Sunday name.

PC JENKINS   Sunday name?

PREMPEH   On Sundays—

DC HARRISON   OK, *Prommy,* can we get back to the matter at hand?

MS. FLINN   Please.

PREMPEH   Well, Uncle Winston opened the cupboard door, and just as he was greeting me in my language, because he saw at once that I was a Kumasi Scout from Ejisu, and in Ghana, sir, we always call our seniors "Uncle"

	and we say *"Ete sen"* and then you answer *"Eyee,"* which means—
DC HARRISON	The MATTER AT HAND, Prempeh!
PREMPEH	Well, sir, Uncle Winston didn't see RollerBoy and HeartofFire, and I'd also got a few of the others lined up in ranks. I call them the Infantry, just like Lord Baden-Powell had infantry when he marched his army into Kumasi.
PC JENKINS	And?
PREMPEH	He slipped, sir. He trod on the marbles and he fell over, and that's when he bumped his head, sir.
MS. FLINN	Try not to worry, Prommy, dear; it was an accident. It wasn't your fault that Mr. Owusu fractured his skull and tore his shoulder ligaments when he fell. He'll be fine. When he gains consciousness, we'll interview him. I'm sure he'll say you're telling the truth.

TAPE STOPPED WHILE MS. FLINN REASSURES PREMPEH. PREMPEH CRIES.

*   *   *

43

DC HARRISON	Let's get this clear. After Mr. Owusu fell, you took his security equipment.
PREMPEH	I just wanted to go and fetch help for Uncle Winston, sir. I didn't mean to unlock all the doors in the Jewel House.
DC HARRISON	How *exactly* did you accomplish that?
PREMPEH	I'm not a thief, sir, or a murderer. I didn't try to kill Uncle Winston, and I would never try to steal the Crown Jewels. That's against the law, sir. Oh, dear, the other boys always said I'd get into trouble one of these days.
MS. FLINN	That's all right, Prommy, but just tell the detective constable how you managed to open every door in the Jewel House and get past the high-tech laser security system and the thermal-imaging alarm sensors.
PC JENKINS	Blimey.
PREMPEH	Well, at the first door — I think it was the first door — this voice thing asked me a question, and I thought it said *"Ete sen"* so I said *"Eyee"* back, and then it said something like *"Oyez,"*

and the door just opened. I forget how I got through the next one, but I was playing with the numbers on the code and trying Uncle Winston's keys and his swipe thing, and I was flicking that blue light on and off, and it really wasn't very hard. I didn't break anything, I hope.

DC HARRISON   Correct me if I'm mistaken, but are you asserting that you advanced through ten security barriers *all* by yourself?

PREMPEH   I did, sir. Lord Baden-Powell says all Scouts have to BE PREPARED. I wasn't very prepared, sir, or I'd have known about first aid, but I was prepared to go for help. Please don't tell Mr. Acheampong that I wasn't prepared, will you, sir?

DC HARRISON   So you just sailed through the most secure stronghold in the whole of the United Kingdom single-handed?

PREMPEH   I didn't sail, sir, I just walked, really. But I did get stuck in one room.

DC HARRISON   Oh? Surprise, surprise!

PREMPEH   It's true, sir. I couldn't go on, or back,

so I thought, *What shall I do?* And when I don't know what to do, I have a little game of marbles. The other boys always laugh and say I should get a PS3 or something, but you can't carry one of those around in your pocket, can you, sir? So I put my marbles down on the floor, just to roll them a little bit, because I thought it wouldn't matter too much—I mean, just a little roll while I was stuck and waiting—and Heart-ofFire rolled a really long way and I followed it. I was wriggling along on my tummy and—

DC HARRISON   You mean you bypassed all the UV scanners in the Antechamber—the ones that automatically lock down the entire building—just by wriggling along the floor on your tummy?

PREMPEH   Did I, sir? I don't know.

MR. OBE, SOLICITOR FOR THE DEFENDANT, AND MR. NARNOR, SECRETARY OF STATE FROM THE GHANA HIGH COMMISSION, ENTER THE INTERVIEW ROOM.

*   *   *

PC JENKINS [*aside*]   Incredible, isn't it? What a kid!

DC HARRISON [*aside*] Rubbish. There's no way that child could have done it on his own. There's somebody else behind all this.

MS. FLINN   You're doing very well, Prommy. Would you like a drink?

PREMPEH   Yes, please.

MS. FLINN LEAVES THE ROOM.

DC HARRISON   So, Prempeh, what occurred after you obtained entry to the Jewel Room? How did you manage to knock out three police officers and cause grievous bodily harm to a fourth?

MR. OBE   You're putting words into the mouth of my client.

PREMPEH   It was an accident, sir. But you see, when I was in the Jewel Room, I wanted to look at the Crown Jewels, because Lord Baden-Powell was interested in the Crown Jewels, and that was because of the biggest jewel of all, the one that's called the Cobbler-or-more, a bit like a marble . . .

PC JENKINS	Koh-i-noor.
PREMPEH	That's it, sir.
PC JENKINS	It means Mountain of Light.
PREMPEH	Like HeartofFire?
PC JENKINS	When I was a lad, we had marbles called—
DC HARRISON	Ahem!
PC JENKINS	You had better get on with your story, son.
PREMPEH	Well, before Lord Baden-Powell was a lord, he came on holiday to Ghana. And that's where he heard about the Golden Stool. And then he had an idea, like his friends had done in India about that Koh-i-noor jewel. His idea was to add the Golden Stool to the Crown Jewels. If you can get precious things for your country like that, sir, you get turned into a lord. The Golden Stool, you see, is like the Crown Jewels of the Ashanti nation, sir. It's this big golden throne, so that's why Mr. Baden-Powell had to attack Kumasi, because he wanted to get it, and sit on it, and get turned into a lord.

DC HARRISON	Lord help me!
PREMPEH	If I were a lord I would help you, sir, and I would probably get all my Scout badges—even the Observer badge, and that's very hard, sir. And I would quite like to sit on the Golden Stool—
DC HARRISON	Stick to the point, boy!
MR. NARNOR	The attempted theft of the Golden Stool, plus Baden-Powell's reprehensible, brutal, and illegal attack on the city of Kumasi, perhaps illustrates a *point* that the boy *is* trying to make.
MR. OBE	And my client has the right to tell his story without continual interruption.
PREMPEH	They never let him sit on it, anyway, although he still got to be a lord! A lady called Yaa Asantewaa led an army of old ladies against Lord-to-Be Baden-Powell and hid the Golden Stool, so when Lord-to-Be Baden-Powell conquered Kumasi, they had to make another golden stool for him to sit on, and that's when they made him a lord.

**MS. FLINN RE-ENTERS THE INTERVIEW ROOM
WITH A CAN OF SODA.**

PREMPEH   I would really like to be a lord.

PREMPEH HAS A SHORT REFRESHMENT BREAK.

DC HARRISON   If you are quite finished, perhaps you
                 can continue *uninterrupted* with the
                 matter in question . . .
PREMPEH   Yes, sir, of course, sir. It's quite simple,
                 sir, because when I saw those Crown
                 Jewels, I thought, *What would Lord
                 Baden-Powell do if he were here
                 now instead of me?* And I thought,
                 *He'd try to get them, just like he
                 tried to get the Golden Stool.* Well, I
                 want to be a good Scout and earn all
                 my badges very quickly, so I thought
                 I'd better do like Lord Baden-Powell
                 did, and I tried everything I could:
                 the swipe, the keys, and the laser
                 flasher.
DC HARRISON   The laser flasher?
PREMPEH   Yes, it was in Uncle Winston's pocket,
                 and I just took it along to help

me get out, so I could help Uncle Winston.

DC HARRISON	You removed it from his pocket.
PREMPEH	Not really, sir. It fell out of his pocket when he hit his head. I was flashing it around, and the case with the biggest crown got opened. I was a bit scared, but that crown was all glittering just like fire, so I thought it might be fun if I put it on, like Lord Baden-Powell had wanted to sit on the Golden Stool . . . Can you be made a lord twice, sir?
DC HARRISON	You removed the laser coder from Mr. Owusu's pocket?
MR. OBE	Please do not intimidate my client.
PREMPEH	I was just doing my best to be like my hero, sir. I took the crown out of the case and I put it on, and then I saw that HeartofFire had rolled and touched RollerBoy, and that's a Double-or-Die move! So I sat down on the floor to finish the game of marbles. When it's Double-or-Die, you have to use all the Infantry, and there were marbles all over the floor,

and I decided to take a photo of me wearing the crown finishing Double-or-Die to show the other boys. They don't normally think I'm cool, sir, but they'll be impressed when they see that! Anyway, that's when the officers burst in. I jumped up and accidentally knocked the crown off. It fell on the floor and some of the jewels might have got loosened. I was worried about that, and the police skidded on the marbles just like Uncle Winston and then fell over. I scooped all the marbles up, and I put the crown back on—well, you know about the lord thing, sir—and I'm pretty sure none of the jewels fell out.

DC HARRISON

What about the officer who received a marble shot to the head?

MS. FLINN

Try not to worry, Prommy. They say his eye can be saved with surgery.

DC HARRISON

And if they can't save his eye, he'll have your guts for garters and your liver with onions, m'boy.

PREMPEH	I'm terribly sorry about that, sir. It wasn't meant to hit him in the face. You see, when you finish Double-or-Die, you have to shoot your best marbles up into the air; it's called a Whoopee Too and it's quite hard, and you have to do it with a lot of force.
DC HARRISON	So you claim that the concussion, broken tibia, and fractured femur sustained by three officers, respectively, plus the serious injury to a fourth and Mr. Owusu's fall, were all accidents?
PREMPEH	Yes, sir.
DC HARRISON	And that is how you came to be wearing Her Majesty's Crown Jewels at the time of your discovery?
PREMPEH	Yes, sir.
DC HARRISON	And have you anything further to say?
PREMPEH	Yes, sir.
DC HARRISON	Well?
PREMPEH	Do I get to be made a lord now, sir?
DC HARRISON	I have never—

MR. OBE The boy has a point. The law should
be the same for all, lord or not. It
should treat everyone fairly.

Signature: *Prommy Prempeh*

Witnessed by: Cato Jenkins

Postscript: On receipt of bail and following the repossession of effects confiscated at the time of arrest, a complaint has been lodged by the Solicitor for the Defendant, *I. Obe, QC,* that one of *Prempeh*'s marbles does not roll as well as the rest, and *Prempeh* wonders if he is entitled to compensation.

ARTICLE 7
THE LAW IS THE SAME FOR EVERYONE. IT MUST TREAT US ALL FAIRLY.

SARSAPARILLA

Ursula Dubosarsky

There was a man who went around slandering a rabbi's good name. One day, feeling guilty and realizing that his loose words had now spread far and wide, he wondered what he should do. So he went to the rabbi and told him what had happened. The rabbi listened to the man, then shook his head sadly.

"This is what I will tell you to do," said the rabbi. "Take this pillow and cut it open. Then go to the open window and toss out all the feathers."

The man did as he was told and then returned to the rabbi.

"Good," said the rabbi. "Now go collect all the feathers and put them back in the pillow."

Traditional Jewish tale

ONE night, Rosabel had a dream about a giant guinea pig. It had soft white fur a bit like an Arctic fox's, pink eyes, and alarmingly long fishing-line whiskers that stretched out way beyond where her (dreaming) eyes could see. But most disconcerting was the expression on its face, as though it could say something very interesting, even important, if it chose to. Was it about to? Unfortunately Rosabel was woken by the rain coming in her open window, and the cold wind. She sneezed, and the dream was over.

"I had a dream last night," Rosabel said on the bus to school that morning.

But nobody wants to hear about other people's dreams: what could be more boring? And none of her friends—well, not really *friends*; travelling companions, more like—expressed the slightest interest in hearing about Rosabel's dream. In fact, one of these companions even quite deliberately turned his head towards the window and stared out at the dull wet street rather than hear about it.

But when she arrived home that afternoon, she realized she should have told him. She should have insisted, pulled him by the shoulder, and shaken him and said, "You *will* hear me! You must!" Because when she turned the corner into her street, there was a man in a dark grey suit sitting on the stone wall in front of her house. He held a large paper bag in his hands, tied at the neck with a rubber band.

The man stood up as she passed and said with some

irritation, "At last! I've come to talk to you about Sarsa-parilla!"

Rosabel gave the man an uneasy smile, then politely averted her eyes. He didn't exactly look like a door-to-door salesman of unusual soft drinks, but she supposed that was what he must be. *I don't even like sarsaparilla,* she thought as she remembered the unpleasantly bitter dark-coloured drink she had tasted once on holiday. *I've got absolutely nothing to say about it, and I certainly don't want to buy any.* In any case, she was not in the habit of talking to strangers, even well-dressed and almost elderly strangers like this man, who managed to give the impression of being rather strange and yet very respectable at the same time. A bit like her school principal, really.

She made her way to her front door, looking intently down at the pathway, where a trail of small brown ants was journeying patiently towards the doorstep. *It must be going to rain,* she said to herself in a bright, silent voice, trying to block out the man's presence, thinking instead of the ants that would soon be crawling into the house, up the kitchen cupboards towards the open sugar bowl.

But to her horror—that is a strong word, but it was a kind of mild horror she felt—as she groped around in her crumb-filled pocket for her key, she became aware that the man with the paper bag was standing right behind her, clicking his tongue impatiently. And worse, as she turned the key and pushed the door open, the man and his paper bag came right inside after her, so forcefully that she had to step out of the way to let him through.

"You should leave a key under the mat," he said. "*Tut-tut.* Then I could have let myself in."

Why is this happening? Rosabel wondered, panicking. Did she know this man? Was he a friend of her mother's whom she had been introduced to and had somehow forgotten?

"So," said the man, straightening his shocking crimson tie. "I'll just sit down and put my feet up, then we can have a good old chat about Sarsaparilla."

"Mum?" called Rosabel, running—well, walking very quickly—into the living room, pretending that her mother was home, even though she knew she was not. Where was she? Visiting someone? Working? What exactly had her mother said that morning over breakfast? Strangely, Rosabel could recall the smell of the slightly burnt toast but not her mother's words.

The man followed her and sat himself down on the sofa, the paper bag on his lap. Then, as though revising his first thought, he put the bag very carefully on the seat next to him. It began to move. *Rustle, really,* Rosabel thought to herself—rather stupidly, as this wasn't the time to be worrying about the right word to describe the movements of a paper bag.

The man stood up. Heading into the kitchen, he said, "I'll just get myself a sandwich."

Well, make yourself at home, thought Rosabel with some indignation.

Which he did. What a mess. He left the peanut butter jar open on the worktop, and flies began to buzz over it.

"Can you come back later?" she said desperately. "When my mother's here?"

"Oh, I'd prefer not to speak to your mother," the man replied, swallowing his last mouthful. "It's a simple matter, after all." He paused and laid down the crusts. He leant on the worktop with his elbow and gave Rosabel a rueful smile. "I seem to be in a bit of bother, you see." He stared at Rosabel, waiting for an answer.

"Oh, dear," she murmured, somehow unable to remain silent.

"And all over a word. Just a little word," said the man, apparently encouraged by her response—or perhaps he didn't need much encouragement. "Really, things can be taken too seriously, don't you think? I mean"—bringing his face close to hers—"what do *you* think of the name Sarsaparilla?"

"Um," said Rosabel, stepping backwards. "I don't know. Really."

"Of course it's not a *good* name." The man nodded, as though agreeing with her. "It's not a name anyone would *want* to have. But it was just a joke. I mean, if a person can't have a bit of fun . . ." He smiled confidently at Rosabel. "And after all, it's just a guinea pig we're talking about here."

Rosabel gulped. A wave of something rolled in her head.

"A guinea pig?" she said faintly.

"Yes, didn't I say?" said the man, returning to the living room and sitting back down on the sofa and crossing his legs.

In Rosabel's dream the eyes of the huge white guinea pig had meaningfully fixed on hers, with a disturbing mixture of emotion and intelligence. But those were not the eyes gazing at her now. Now it was the man's eyes, round, glistening, the colour of watermelon rind.

"I painted it—rather beautifully, may I say—on the front of her cage," he went on, pushing the quivering paper bag a little further along the sofa. "Lovely golden letters— **Sarsaparilla.** Helvetica Bold, you know. My favourite font."

The man was clearly some kind of nut, Rosabel decided—which was not comforting.

"You put a sign on the cage?" she asked, just to make sure she had understood him. "Saying *Sarsaparilla*?"

"Oh, I took it down straight away," the man replied quickly. "It's gone now."

"But . . ." Rosabel faltered. "I mean . . . why?"

To her alarm the man leapt to his feet, irritated.

"Well, why *not*? Why shouldn't I say what I think?" He frowned at Rosabel severely. "I've got the right to my opinion, haven't I? She looked exactly like a Sarsaparilla to me!"

"Oh," said Rosabel, taken aback. "I thought you said it was just a joke—that you didn't really mean it—"

"A joke! Well, I hope we haven't come to a point where we're afraid to speak our minds." The man stood rigidly to attention, like a soldier. "What a sorry state of affairs that would be. Censorship. Do you know what that means? Now *that's* a crime, stopping people from speaking out. Freedom is above all!"

"But if it isn't actually her name . . ." said Rosabel helplessly. If she could just somehow get him to leave! Maybe if she pretended she had to go out herself?

The man slumped back down on the sofa again. "Who cares, anyway?" he muttered. "I wouldn't care if someone called me Sarsaparilla."

The rustling became louder. The bag even seemed to shuffle a little towards him. Rosabel blinked, and the thought occurred to her at last. Had he actually brought the guinea pig with him?

"I don't think," she said in a small, nervous, yet firm voice, "that I would like to be called Sarsaparilla if it wasn't my name."

He gave her a short smile and lowered his eyelids. "Ah, my dear, as the poet says: 'What's in a name?' et cetera, et cetera. 'A rose by any other name,' you know. Ever heard of Shakespeare?"

"Actually, I don't think that's true," began Rosabel, irritated, because *of course* she had heard of Shakespeare, but the man wasn't interested and had now fully closed his eyes. Was he going to fall asleep?

Then, as though he could hear her thoughts, he roused himself, opened his eyes, and leant towards her, confidential and devious.

"You must understand, there are more important things at stake here than a mere guinea pig," he hissed. "We must use such weapons as we can. So what if I lied? So what if she looks absolutely nothing like a Sarsaparilla? What does that matter? That's not what's at stake, is it?"

The bag shook urgently.

"Anyway," said the man, ignoring the bag and stroking the smooth surface of his tie, "what do a few simple lies matter if they get us what we want? There's no law against lying."

Rosabel was mystified. "But, I mean . . ." *Weren't* there laws against lying? If there weren't, wasn't that just because everybody knew it was wrong? After all, on the train there were signs telling you it was forbidden to put your feet on the seats, to drink alcohol, and all that sort of thing. You didn't need signs saying it was forbidden to commit murder or to tell lies about someone. Everyone knew it was wrong to do that. Didn't they? Rosabel glanced down at the bag, then stared at it. There was definitely something alive in there.

The man yawned and blinked at the ceiling. The bag was crackling now, as though something was straining to get out.

"What's her name, anyway?" Rosabel asked suddenly, looking up. "The guinea pig. Her real name?"

"Ah." The man glanced at his watch. "It's hard to remember now. Once the word *Sarsaparilla* gets into your head — well, it sticks, doesn't it?"

Perhaps it was because of her dream, but Rosabel felt an anger rising in her on behalf of that guinea pig. To take someone's name away like that, so willfully, was like — what was it like? It was like going into a person's house and searching around for something special — *like my little apple,* she thought, catching sight of the china apple they kept on the shelf. Her mother had given it to her for her sixth birthday, and Rosabel loved it. It probably didn't look like much to anyone else, but to her it was special. It was as though this man had walked into her house, picked up the little apple, and smashed it with a hammer.

The man stood up, clearly preparing to leave.

"Anyway," he added. "Luckily guinea pigs don't live very long."

He put on his hat with one hand and with the other seized the paper bag from the sofa. He thrust it towards Rosabel. "Hang on to this for me, will you?" he said. "Maybe you can do something about it. I've had enough."

Then he strode down the hallway, flung open the front door, and was gone.

Me? thought Rosabel. *But what can I do? I don't know anything about guinea pigs!*

A great gust of wind came pouring through the open front door. The bag fell out of Rosabel's shocked grip onto the floor, and the rubber band that was holding its contents tight inside snapped.

Aghast, Rosabel watched as out of the mouth of the bag came not, as she had suspected, a frightened guinea pig, but instead a stream of tiny white feathers. Feathers! As though Sarsaparilla had been transformed from her own self into hundreds—no, thousands—of shreds of random whiteness. The feathers flew upwards in the wind and outwards in a mysterious, determined cloud, right out of the front door.

"Help!" cried Rosabel, running after them onto the pavement. "Sarsaparilla!" She snatched desperately at the feathers, but they slipped through her fingers like tiny silver fish in a vast cold ocean.

Where was the man who had caused all the trouble? It wasn't fair. What had *she* done? *He should be the one running after the terrible swirling mass,* she thought, *not me.* In any case, it was too late now, too late to do anything.

"Sarsaparilla!"

Rosabel looked wildly up and down the street. It was empty, deserted except for a small boy who was sitting on the stone wall in front of her house, his school cap on his head and his bag on his back, eating a pink iced bun.

The child looked curiously at Rosabel, then up at the shoal of feathers, now dancing in all directions above their heads.

"That's pollution," he remarked, licking the icing from his bun. "What are you going to do?"

And Rosabel gazed up at the sky in a kind of fathomless dismay. The specks of white grew smaller and smaller, disappearing at last as they floated relentlessly into the wide world, and she realized that in fact she could do nothing at all.

ARTICLE 12

NOBODY SHOULD TRY TO HARM OUR GOOD NAME. NOBODY HAS THE RIGHT TO COME INTO OUR HOME, OPEN OUR LETTERS, OR BOTHER US OR OUR FAMILY WITHOUT A VERY GOOD REASON.

Author's Note

This is a story about a guinea pig. You might think, What does a guinea pig have to do with human rights? *Well, sometimes when I'm writing, I find I can think better if I imagine I'm writing about something else altogether (some people call this a metaphor). I think human rights are about protecting the small and powerless, who find it hard to stick up for themselves. And we've probably all felt like a small and powerless guinea pig ourselves at some time in our lives.*

AFTER THE HURRICANE

Rita Williams-Garcia

If toilets flushed,
if babies slept,
if faucets ran,
old bodies didn't die in the sun,
if none of it were real,
if we weren't in it,
this could be a disaster movie with
helicopters whipping up sky overhead,
Special Effects brought in to create Lake George
      and not the great Mississippi
        meeting Lake Pontchartrain.
Out-of-work waiters would pose as policemen,
locals as extras paid in box lunches.
For set design, dump raw sewage, trash everywhere,
news trucks, patrol cars, army tanks, Humvees.

If none of it were real,
if we weren't in it,
this could be a big-budget disaster flick
King, Jasper, and I'd rent
after band practice
like we did last Tuesday watching *Titanic* on Grandmama's
sofa.
That Jasper could *laaaugh* at all the actors drowning
while the band played—*glub, glub, glub*—to the death.

But this ain't that. We're waist high in it.
Camera crews bark, "Big Mike! Get this, over here!"
"Roll tape."
"Got that?"
"Good God!"
"Shut it down."

This ain't hardly no picture.
We're not on location.
We're herded. Domed in,
feels like for good
unless you caught a bus like Ma
or Jasper's family (save Jasper).
I still want to smash a camera,
break a lens, make them stop shooting.

But King says, "No, Freddie. Gotta show it.
Who'd believe it without film?"

Still no running water, no food, no power, no help.
The world is here but no one's coming.
The Guard is here with rifles pointed.
The Red Cross got their tables set up.
Weathermen, anchors, reporters, meteorologists,
a fleet of black Homeland SUVs.
The world is here
but where is the water? The food? The power?
The way to Ma or Jasper's people.
They just herd us, split us, film us, guard us.
No one said feed us. No one brought water.
The world is here but no one's coming.
Helicopters overhead beat up on our skies.

*   *   *

Miracle One.
King noses around the news guys,
runs back to Jasper and me.
"There's water trucks held up on the highway.
Gallons, girl! Water by the gallons.
Fresh drinking water.
Clean shower water.

See that, Freddie. The water company loves us.
Somebody thought to send us water."
Even with our trumpets drowned, King's chest swells.
He booms, "Brass Crew, are you with me?
Let's get outta here, bring back some water."

How can I leave TK and Grandmama?
How can I leave, and be happy to leave?
Watch me. Just watch me
high step on outta here
for the water I say I'll bring back.
Honest to God, I heard "Brass Crew" and was gone.
I heard *Elbows up,*
natural breath!
That was enough.
How can I leave, and be happy to leave?
Easy. As needing to breathe new air.

King's got a First Trumpet stride. Jasper walks.
I lick the salt off my bare arms,
turn to look back at the people
held up by canes, hugging strollers, collapsible
black and newly colored people,
women with shirts for head wraps.
Salt dries my tongue.
I turn my eyes from them and walk.

I don't have to tell myself
it's not a school project for Ms. LeBlanc,
"The Colored Peoples of Freddie's Diorama."
Green pasted just so, around the huts just so.
The despair just right.
It's not my social studies diorama
depicting "Over There," across the Atlantic,
the Pacific. Bodies of water.
Way, way over there.
The refugees of the mudslides,
refugees of the tsunami,
refugees of Rwanda.
No. It is US. In state. In country.
Drowned but not separated by
bodies of water or by spoken language.
The despair is just right, no translation needed.
We are not the refugees in my social studies diorama.
We are 11th graders,
a broken brass line,
old homeowners, grandmamas, head chefs, street
performers, a saxophonist mourning the loss of his Selmer
horn of 43 years and wife of 38 years. We are aunties,
dry cleaners, cops' daughters, deacons, cement mixers,
auto mechanics, trombonists without trombones, quartets
scattered, communion servers, stranded freshmen, old
nuns, X-ray technicians, bread bakers, curators, diabetics,

71

shrimpers, dishwashers, seamstresses, brides-to-be, new
daddies, taxi drivers, principals, Cub Scouts crying, car
dealers, other dealers, hairstylists, too many babies, too
many of us to count.
Still wearing what we had on when it hit.
When we fled,
or were wheeled, piggybacked, airlifted, carried off.
Citizens herded.
We are Ms. LeBlanc, social studies teacher, a rag wrapped
around her head,
And Principal Canelle. He missed that last bus.

*　　*　　*

Minor Miracle.
We walk past the Guard.
You'd think they'd see us
marching on outta here.
You'd think they'd stop us. Keep us domed.
But we're on the march, a broken brass line.
King, Jasper, and me, Fredericka.

King needs to lead; I need to leave.
Been following his lead since
band camp. Junior band. Senior band.
Box formations, flying diamonds, complicated transitions.
Jasper sticks close. A horn player, a laugher. Not a talker.

See anything to laugh about?
Jasper sticks close. Stays quiet. Maybe a nod.

Keeping step I would ask myself,
Aren't you ashamed? No.
Of band pride? No.
You band geek. So.
Aren't you ashamed? No.
You want to parade? So.
Raise your trumpet? So.
Aren't you ashamed? No.
To praise Saint Louis?
"Oh, when the saints go marching in?"
Aren't you ashamed? No.
Of strutting krewe
On Mardi Gras? The Fourth of July?
These very streets
Purple and gold, bop
Stars and Stripes, bop
Aren't you ashamed?
To shake and boogie?
Aren't you ashamed?
To enjoy your march,
while Grandmama suffers
and no milk for TK?
Tell the truth. Aren't you ashamed?

No. I'm not ashamed.
I step high, elbows up.
Band pride.

King asks, "Freddie, what you thinking?"
I say, "I'm not thinking, King."
But I'm dried out on the inside.
Hungry talks LOUD, you know.
"Let's try the Beauxmart. The Food Circle. Something."

King knows better. He doesn't say.
Still, we go and find (no surprise)
the Beauxmart's been hit. Stripped. Smashed.
Forget about Food Circle and every corner grocery.
Nothing left but rotten milk,
glass shards. Loose shopping carts.
Jasper sighs. Grabs a cart.

Stomach won't shut up.
Talking. Knotting. Cramping. I whine,
"Let's go to Doolie's."
Again, King knows better. Still, we go,
almost passed right by. Didn't see it until
Jasper points. King sighs.
Check out the D in Doolie's, blown clear off.
The outside boarded up, chained up, locked.

Black and red spray-painted:
LOOTERS WILL BE SHOT.

I can't believe it.
Doolie who buys block tickets to home games
Doolie who sponsors our team bus
Band instruments, uniforms (all underwater),
Chicken bucket championships. The band eats half-price.
My eyes say, *Freddie, believe the spray paint:*
Big Sean Doolie will shoot the looters.
Yeah. Big Sean Doolie.
Believe.

King (First Trumpet) was right,
he doesn't make me (Second) like I'm second.
A simple, "Come on, Brass. Let's get this water."
I follow King. Jasper pushes the cart.
First, Second, Third. No bop step,
high step, no feather head shake,
no shimmy front, boogie back.
Just walk.

"Hear that?"
Another helicopter overhead.
Another chopper stirring up the Big Empty.
Wide blades good for nothing but whirling up

75

heavy heat, heavy stink on empty streets
full of ghosts and mosquitoes.
Swat all you want. Look around.
Nothing here but us in Big Empty.

*   *   *

Miracle Two.
A blue-and-white stands pit-bull stiff.
Helmet. Radio. Rifle. Ready.
Holds up the barrel, points to the dome.
"You can't pass here. Get on that way."

King keeps coming.
We come with King.
"No," he says. *"That's"*—finger points—"where we came
from."

The blue-and-white steadies his barrel.
"Then you know"—chin points—"the way back."

King believes in the law, uniforms, and simple reason.
Even during these times
King believes the law can see his invisible uniform
(chest puffed out like he's Some Body).
King believes the law can follow simple reason. "Officer,
there's water trucks on the highway. They came here for us."

76

Maybe it's tone.
King has good tone.
Maybe it's his invisible uniform.
I see, believe, and add, "We have babies and grandmamas
at the dome, needing water."
Jasper, a convert, nods. King cajoles, reasons,
"Come on, chief. The water. The water. Let us pass."

The po-po says, "Listen, you looters—"
But his radio cuts in.
It's a crisis. *(And this isn't?)*
"See the looters on Royal. Stop the looters.
Stop the gall-darned looters."
The blue-and-white tears off, red lights whirl,
sirens scream, "Crisis! Crisis! Shoe store in crisis!"

Hail Mary, we pass on through.

Feeling the faith, I say,
"Black Moses of Walker Rawlins High,
go 'head, King. Tap a rock.
A big rock, a cinder block. Go 'head, Black Moses,
make the water shoot out."
For half a second King grins.
We've stumbled on a Way and can't be turned back.

I give a side glance.

Used to be easy to set off Jasper's
firecracker laugh. Before this,
any lame joke could light him up,
crack open that mouth, ripple his red berry tongue.
But this ain't no occasion.
You can't jolly Jasper.
It's not right to try.

*   *   *

On the march we meet a ragtag band,
not a matched sock between them.
Just folks taking turns
as eyes, worriers, arms, and crutches
leading each other.
A young guy pushes an old white woman
in a wheelchair.
A black girl my age holds a Chinese baby.
A petless man has three dogs and a cat.
Mismatch adoption sure looks easy.
I wonder if Ma's lap is full.

"Don't go to Gretna," says the old-lady pusher.
"They turning them back, black or white."
"Stay off that bridge."

"Don't go that way. It's all cut off."
"Blocked off's more like it."
"Only one way they'll let you pass.
Only one way they'll point you."
"Be careful 'round here.
They shooting looters."

King says, "Naw, naw. We're here for water.
We're not looters."
A mouth full of gold laughs back.
"You not looters. Neither am I."
His cart loaded down. "All the same,
y'all be careful."

Their krewe splits right.
We press on.

I follow King.
Jasper pushes our empty cart.
I say, "Don't worry, Jasper. We'll all
push it back—full as we plan on filling it!"
Easier to take turns pushing twenty gallons
than return to the dome without a drop.

Looters gotta worry; we just want water.
Water, not flat screens,

Water, not cell phones,
Water, not Gucci bags.
Stupid diamond wristwatch? (*spit*) Please.
But if bread's on the way, Hungry says, "It's on!"
Can't outtalk Hungry when Hungry's loud as hell.
Surely no one'll shoot you for a loaf of dry bread.

*   *   *

I miss the drum line
and start to fill in,
"Pontchartrain
Mississippi
and not a drop to drink."

Then King says, "Freddie. What you humming?"
I say it out loud.
Soon King joins me.
"Pontchartrain
Mississippi
and not a drop to drink."

Our line song don't interest Jasper
but he sure likes the pace.
We pick it up, feeling we're getting closer.
"Pontchartrain
Mississippi

and not a drop to drink."

We keep marching, pushing
King and I battle-hymning
like Walker Rawlins Gators
with the ball on the twenty.
Who needs a touchdown in a
crumbling dome when
we can score water?
Just a half mile and goal to go.
Aah.
I dream of shower walking,
holding a jug overhead,
letting her spill.

We're close. Close like
birds sent out from sea
to circle land.
It's true about being out to sea
and being close.

"Eyes, am I seeing things?"
A sand mirage in the desert.
Is that our caravan lined up to greet us?
I rub my eyes. Could just be the sweat.

*   *   *

Come on, Major Miracle.
Chest out, cart ready, we roll on
to meet our prayer truck.
As always, First Trumpet takes the first step.
We keep up, Second and Third.

It's clear.
We see their camouflage,
jeeps, tanks. A war-colored Humvee
on our streets.
No one sees King's brass buttons, epaulets, tassels,
invisible or drowned along with ours.
No one knows King dreams of marching
for Army
in the Army versus Navy fall classic.
That he'll spit-shine his horn until the bell blinds.

King raises his hand (to point).
They raise rifles, M16s, AKs—I don't know guns—
on target.

Two Bars on Helmet barks, "Halt! You can't pass here."
So we don't move.
I'm stopped.
Jasper's stopped.
But King still believes: law, uniform, simple reason.

"Sir, we just need—"
The crack of M16s or AKs—I don't know guns—
stiffen the air.
Two Bars says, "No one passes through this checkpoint."

I'm like Jasper:
Stopped. Silent. Scared. Enraged.
My silent words shout:
This isn't your guardhouse.
You're not our Guard.
These are our streets.
We've marched here in full dress,
White gloves, high itchy hats,
carrying brass, drums, batons, flags,
Waving our colors
across the river and back.
Checkpoint?
Stop us at the checkpoint?
But my eyes say, *Believe, Freddie.*
They're squinting to shoot.

While King tries simple reason
my silent words won't shut up:
They will block us
off our own streets
raise rifles—guns—on

our parade route.
This isn't colors versus colors,
a battle of the
high school bands.
Faith long deserted, my
eyes say, Believe, Freddie.
The Guard will shoot.

Two Bars says,
"I don't care what's on the other side.
No one gets past this checkpoint."
Two Bars says,
"Turn back or be shot."

King stands. Lets out a natural breath.
A second too long to know
what Jasper and I been knowing:
No more Hail Mary passes.
Simple reason, invisible band uniforms, the law
don't fly at the checkpoint.
King stands. Lets out a natural breath
A second too long.

Two Bars gives the order.
Rifles, M16s, AKs—guns—respond.
A spray of cracks and BOOMs overhead.

Another BOOM-BOOM-BOOM.
BOOM-BOOM-BOOM
over our heads.

My bowels and legs buckle.
Collapsible, I'm the first to fold. No cane,
just King and Jasper around me.
Gather me. Lift me.
In the cart.
King pushes behind Jasper.

*   *   *

On the way back to the dome
they find a place for me to dump.
They turn. I squat—nothing left. Still, I push.
After, I say, "I'm good. Just let me walk."
So we leave the cart and walk.

At first nothing.
Silence.
Not even choppers overhead.
Then firecrackers set off loud in my ear.
Firecrackers choking up,
not like on Grandmama's sofa
while watching *Titanic,*
but sparklers, cherry bombs, bursting loud in my ear.

"Ahaaaaaa . . . Haaaa (*choke*) Haaaa!"
Jasper laughs, at last: "Trucks full of water
on Highway 90
and not one of us can cross.
Water, water everywhere
and not one drop to drink.
Only in the land of the free.
Only in America."

ARTICLE 13

WE ALL HAVE THE RIGHT TO GO WHERE WE WANT TO IN OUR OWN COUNTRY AND TO TRAVEL ABROAD AS WE WISH.

Author's Note

In August 2005, Hurricane Katrina hit the south coast of the United States, causing one of the greatest natural disasters in the nation's history. Worst affected was the city of New Orleans in the state of Louisiana, and many felt that the extensive loss of life in this city could have been avoided had the government responded more quickly to the plight of its people.

IF ONLY PAPA
HADN'T DANCED

Patricia McCormick

BUT who could blame him? When the results of the presidential election were tacked up on the polling-station doors, a lot of people danced and sang in the streets—none of them more joyfully than Papa. Finally the Old Man had lost. The Old Man, who'd ruled this country since Papa was a baby, had been beaten fair and square. The man who robbed from the poor to make himself rich was finished.

But not everyone in the village danced that night. The rich men, the ones made fat by the Old Man, stood in the shadows and watched.

The next day, when Papa and his friends gathered around the radio, they heard that the election results had been a mistake. There would have to be a recount. Papa spat in the dust and said it was a lie. A week passed, then another—while the Old Man stayed in his grand house in the capital. While his men were supposedly counting the ballots again. Papa and his friends grumbled among themselves, but not loud enough for anyone else to hear.

Then one night we awoke to the hot breath of fire. The corn patch just outside our hut was ablaze. We jumped from our beds and ran to the field to beat down the flames with branches. But it was no good. Our entire crop was gone.

At dawn Papa sought out the police. They came to our home, looked at our field with eyes of stone, and told us to empty the house of all we owned.

"Take what you can," one of the policemen said. "They will be back tonight. This time they will torch your house."

"They?" I asked Papa when the policemen had left. "Who are 'they'?"

Papa sighed and shook his head. "Our neighbors and tribesmen," he said. "People we have known our whole lives. People whose bellies have been filled by the Old Man."

Mama clucked her tongue at Papa. "Everyone saw you celebrating," she said. "They know you voted against the Old Man, and now we will pay for it." She looked out and saw the smoldering remains of our neighbors' fields. The crops of those who'd danced with Papa were in ashes. The others were as lush and green as they'd been the day before.

And so we packed our things—the few we had, the fewer we could carry—into a few bundles and an old cardboard suitcase. I put my bundle on my head, took one last look at our home, then turned to face our future.

"Where will we go?" I asked Papa.

"We will walk until we find a friendly place where we can stay," he said. "When it is safe, when the recount is finished, when the rightful president takes office, then we will return home."

As we came to the center of the village, we met up with other families like ours. The fathers hung their heads, the mothers looked only at the dirt beneath their feet, and the children tugged listlessly at their parents' hands. "Why?" they asked. "Why must we leave home?" The parents did not dare to answer—in case "they" were listening.

The world beyond the village was new and strange—a vast plain of parched grass and shimmering heat. We walked by night, through bushes alive with the sounds of frenzied insects, and slept by day under the scanty shade of the acacia tree. We walked and walked and walked.

At last we came upon a settlement. From a distance it bloomed up from the earth like a flower. We saw, shimmering on the horizon, what we thought was our safe place, the place where we would rest until we could go home. But as we drew near, we saw that the village looked just like ours. One house was nothing but a smoldering heap, the one next door untouched.

And so we walked on and on, each village the same.

We gathered news as we walked. "The Old Man is still in power," said people who joined our dusty procession. "He won't give up without a fight," they added.

I asked Papa about the man who had won the election. "He won't give up without a fight either," Papa told me. The next day on the radio, we heard that he had fled the country.

That night, there was just one tiny strip of dried meat left. Mama cut it three ways and handed each of us a piece. Papa shook his head.

"Give mine to the child," he said. "I'm a tough old bird. I can make do."

The next morning, when we awoke, we found corn to eat. Corn and biscuits and a bit of fruit. But Papa wouldn't touch a thing. He turned away and whispered to Mama, "I was a fool to hope for change. And now I am a thief. Now I'm no better than the Old Man."

In the afternoon we came upon a great river. Wide and sluggish, it looked as hot and steamy as we were. I knew from my studies that we had come to the edge of our country. On the other side of the river was a free country, a land of cities and farms, a nation where the people had voted for a president who had spent years in jail fighting for justice.

Mama knelt in the shallows and splashed water on her face. But as I knelt down next to her, I saw that she was trying to cover her tears.

"*This* is our homeland," she said. "No one wants us over there." She gestured to the tawny hills across the river.

It was then that I saw the long metal fence that uncoiled, like a snake, all along the riverbank on the other side. The fence was tall and crowned with rings of wire: wire with teeth that could slice the clothes from your back, the skin from your bones. In the distance I saw a man in an orange jumpsuit patching a hole at the bottom of the fence—a spot where some lucky person must have slipped through the night before. His tools were at his feet, a pistol in his belt.

Papa came over and said I was needed. There was a sign, he said, that he needed me to read. He brought me to a spot where someone had hand-painted a warning: *Beware of crocodiles*.

That night, we hid in the bushes until the sky was black. We would wade across at midnight, when the man in the orange jumpsuit had gone home and when the crocodiles, we hoped, would be sound asleep.

When it was time to go, I walked straight toward the river, knowing my nerve would fail if I faltered for even a moment. But Papa stopped me at the water's edge.

"Wait here," he said. And then he scooped Mama up into his arms and waded silently into the darkness.

It seemed a lifetime until he returned. He didn't say a word, just lifted me up onto his shoulders and strode into the water. Every stick I saw was a crocodile. Under every rock, every ripple in the water, was a pair of ferocious jaws. When we reached the other side, I leaped from his shoulders and kissed the sand.

Once more Papa stepped into the river—this time to fetch our suitcase. Surely our luck wouldn't hold again. . . . I watched his back disappear into the dark and thought how much I loved that broad back, how it shouldered all our woes, and now all our hopes. Finally Papa emerged from the darkness with all our worldly possessions balanced on his head.

Then we got down on our hands and knees and crawled along the base of the fence, like scorpions looking for a place to dig. But the sand was unyielding and the fence invincible. Everywhere our fingers scrabbled for a weakness, someone—the man in the orange jumpsuit, most likely—had mended it with links of chain held tight with wire.

The sky overhead had begun to brighten and the horizon was edged with pink. Soon it would be light and we'd be trapped between the waking crocodiles and the man with the gun in his belt.

We came to a spot in the fence where a thorn bush grew on the other side. Papa said we would have to dig here: no time to keep looking. Perhaps the roots of the bush had loosened the sand, he said. If not, at least we could hide behind the bush, if only for a while.

And so all three of us dug—Mama in the middle and Papa and I on either side—our hands clawing furiously at the earth. I'd only made a few inches of progress when the sky turned red. It would be dawn in less than an hour. I redoubled my effort, working the outer edge of the bush where the soil was a bit looser. Soon I'd dug a hole barely big enough for a man's foot. I lifted my head to call out to Papa to come and see my work—and saw the man in the orange jumpsuit striding toward us.

Mama wailed piteously, then plucked at her hem where she'd hidden the tiny bit of money we had. She knelt in the sand, her arms outstretched, our few coins in her upturned palms.

But the man shook his head. He placed his hand on the belt that held his gun.

"Take me," Papa begged him. "Spare the woman and the girl."

Again the man shook his head. Then he reached into his pocket and took out a giant cutting tool. With one mighty snap he severed the links where the fence had been patched. He yanked on the fence so hard it cried out in protest, and peeled it back as if it were made of cloth.

"Hurry," he said. "Once the light comes, I will have to go back to patrolling."

We didn't fully comprehend what he was saying, but we didn't wait.

"You go first," Papa said to me. "I want you to be the first in our family to taste freedom."

I scrambled through the fence, stood next to the man in the orange jumpsuit, and looked back at our homeland as the sun began to turn its fields to gold.

"You will miss it for a long time," the man said to me. "I still do."

I stared up at him.

"Yes," he said. "I outran the Old Man long ago."

Mama crawled through and kissed the man's boots. He simply helped her to her feet.

"Quickly now," he said once Papa had made it through. "Walk, as fast as you can, until you see a house with white flowers out front. Go round to the back and tell them Robert sent you. They will feed you and hide you until night. Then they will send you to the next safe house, which will send you to the next, and the next—until finally you are in the city and can be swallowed up by all the people there."

"How do we know we can trust these people?" Mama asked.

"They are our countrymen," he said. "You will find many of us here. Now go!"

We did as he instructed, and found the house with the white flowers just as the morning sun broke through the clouds. A woman there brought us inside, gave us water and meat, and led us to mats where we could rest. It had been so long since I'd slept on anything other than bare, open ground that I fell asleep at once.

I awoke sometime later and saw that Papa's mat was empty. I stood and wandered outside. The sun was setting, so all I could see was his silhouette against the deepening sky. He raised his arms to the heavens and started to hum. And then I saw Papa dance.

ARTICLE 14
IF WE ARE FRIGHTENED OF BEING BADLY TREATED IN OUR OWN COUNTRY, WE ALL HAVE THE RIGHT TO RUN AWAY TO ANOTHER COUNTRY TO BE SAFE.

Author's Note
In April 2008, tens of thousands of people fled Zimbabwe after a vote that was widely reported to have defeated the sitting president, Robert Mugabe. The ruling party called for a recount and eventually announced that Mugabe

had indeed won the election. After threats against his life, Mugabe's opponent, Morgan Tsvangirai, went into hiding. By then many citizens had fled from mobs intent on attacking and killing those who were alleged to have voted against Mugabe. Thousands streamed across the border to South Africa. Some were given safe haven. Many were attacked and beaten by anti-immigrant groups who feared that the refugees would swamp their country. Some were killed.

PRINCE FRANCIS

Roddy Doyle

IT was very exciting. The whole class was going to be interviewed, as if they were on television. In fact, they *were* on television.

The camera was in position, at the top of the classroom. Daragh was the cameraman.

Francis envied Daragh. He had wanted to be the cameraman. He had put his hand up. "Sir! Sir! Sir, me!" But Sir had chosen Daragh.

That was OK. Francis didn't really mind. He liked Daragh.

"All right," said Sir. *"Ciúnas."*

Francis knew that *ciúnas* meant "quiet" in Irish. He knew some other Irish words too. *Buachaill* meant "boy." And *leithreas* meant "toilet."

"We're all set," said Sir. "Where's our first celebrity?"

They laughed and looked at one another. This was going to be fun.

One of the girls, Alice, was the interviewer. She was wearing a black dress that had once belonged to her grandmother, and black eyeshadow that made her blink. She had a clipboard on her lap, with her questions.

"Kevin," said Sir. "You're first."

Kevin went up to the top of the classroom and sat in the chair beside Alice.

"How's it going, Alice?" he said.

They laughed. Alice blinked.

"OK," said Sir. "Daragh, are we rolling?"

Daragh nodded. "Yes, sir."

"Good man," said Sir. "And . . ."

"Action!" shouted the rest of the class.

"Good evening," said Alice into the camera. "And welcome to *Back Chat*. My name is Alice and this is my first guest."

She was very good, although her blinking was quite strange to look at. It was almost as if she were trying to swim, but using her eyelids instead of her arms.

"What's your name?" she asked.

"Kevvo," said Kevin.

"And where are you from?"

"Here," said Kevin.

"My goodness," said Alice. "You were born in this classroom?"

"No way," said Kevin. "That'd be stupid."

Everyone laughed. Sir was laughing, too.

"Where were you born, then, Mister Kevvo?"

"Outside," said Kevin. "I mean, down the road. I mean—I don't know. In a hospital."

"And what are your interests, Kevvo?"

"Football."

"And?"

"GAA."

"*Gaah?*" said Alice. "What is *gaah?*"

"Gaelic football," said Kevin.

Francis played on the same team as Kevin. He had joined the team when he came to the school, four years ago, when he was seven. He remembered he had been very surprised the first time he'd played, when one of the boys picked up the ball. Handling the ball was permitted in Gaelic football. In fact, handling the ball was important.

Kevin's interview was over. It was Jane's turn. She sat in the chair, in front of Alice. She was wearing a green wig.

"Good evening," said Alice.

"Good morning," said Jane.

"And who are you?"

"Jane."

"Jane," said Alice. "What a lovely name. It rhymes with 'pain.'"

"Take it easy, Alice," warned Sir.

"It's OK," said Jane. "Alice rhymes with 'malice.'"

"And where are *you* from, Pain—sorry—Jane?"

"Ireland," said Jane.

"That explains your green hair."

"Yes," said Jane. "It's the same colour as your snot."

"Hold on!" said Sir. He jumped in front of the camera. "Stop!"

"Do you mean 'cut,' sir?" Daragh asked.

"Yes," said Sir. "Yes. Cut." He turned to the two girls. "Girls," he said.

Francis was surprised by what had happened. Alice and Jane were best friends.

"I was only joking, sir," protested Jane.

"Me as well," said Alice.

"Pain is my nickname, sir," said Jane.

"Yes," said Alice.

Francis wondered if he would ever have a nickname. He hoped so. He had been here four years. He had no enemies, but also no close friends. The other children were quite friendly, but none of them had given him a name that meant strong friendship.

Alice and Jane were ready again.

"And . . ."

"Action!"

"Now, Jane," said Alice. "Tell us a bit about yourself. Tell us about the *real* Jane."

"Well—"

"Do you have a pony?"

"No!"

"What about a donkey?"

Alice was funny. Francis admired her confidence.

"I like Harry Potter," said Jane.

"Oh," said Alice. "Is he your boyfriend?"

Francis had read, so far, three of the Harry Potter books. The lady in the hostel, Mary, had given them to him. He had read each of them twice. There was a small shelf, between his bed and his mother's, that he used for his things. The books were on the shelf, his first books in this country.

Jane stood up, and Derek took her place.

"Hello, you," said Alice.

Sir laughed, and everybody else laughed. Francis could see that Derek was embarrassed.

"Hello," said Derek.

"And you are who?"

"Derek," said Derek.

"Derek," said Alice. "And tell us, Derek, where are you from?"

"The UK," said Derek.

"The what?" said Alice.

Francis was surprised again. He had thought that Derek, like the other children, was Irish. He certainly looked Irish. He was the only person in the class with red hair and freckles.

"Britain," said Derek. "England, like."

"You're English," said Alice.

"I was born there," said Derek. "So, yeah. I suppose." He shrugged.

"How interesting," said Alice. "Why did you come here? To Ireland."

"My dad's Irish," said Derek. "And my mum got a job here. So we moved."

"When?"

"When I was six."

"In a plane?"

"No," said Derek. "Boat."

"Do you remember it?"

"Yeah," said Derek. "'Course. We drove to the boat from our house in London. Then the boat. Then we drove again. To our house here, like."

Francis remembered his own journey here, to Dublin. He had travelled on a train from Belfast, in the north of Ireland—he had seen it since, on a map. But before that, he had been on a plane. Before that, there had been a long wait, in a very hot room with no windows. With his mother. And with many other people. Before that, there had been another plane. And before that, a bumpy journey in the back of a truck, when he lay beside his mother and there was a dusty canvas cover over them and the other people hiding with them. It was very frightening. His mother sang but she sounded frightened, too. Before that, he remembered walking. A long distance, at nighttime. And before that, he remembered running—he thought he did. And gunshots. It was a long time ago; he was not sure.

"Francis?"

Everybody was looking at him. The chair beside Alice was empty. It was Francis's turn.

He stood up. He had been looking forward to this. From where he had been sitting, it had looked like great fun. Now he was not so sure. His legs felt rubbery as he walked to the chair.

"Hurry up, Francis!"

"Quiet," said Sir. "OK, Francis?"

Francis nodded. "Yes, sir."

"Good man. And . . ."

"Action!"

"Good evening," said Alice. She was blinking even faster.

"Good evening," said Francis. He wasn't nervous now.

"And who are *you*?" Alice asked.

Francis waited until the laughter had died down. Then: "Francis," he said, quite loudly.

"Franc*is* or Franc*es*?" said Alice. "Boy or girl?"

"Alice," Sir warned.

"Boy," said Francis.

"Sure?"

"Alice!"

"Very sure," said Francis. "I am, without doubt, a boy."

And something wonderful happened. Everybody laughed. Francis had decided to make his classmates laugh, and he had done it. This was a great day.

Francis laughed, too, then stopped.

"So," said Alice. "You're a boy."

"Yes."

"What sort of a boy?"

"A most ordinary boy."

Again he heard the laughter. Alice blinked and blinked and blinked.

"What's the most ordinary thing about you?" she asked.

"My hands," said Francis. He showed them to her. "And my feet." He held them up, and put them back down on the floor. "I have two of each," he said, "which is very ordinary, I think you will agree."

"Yes," said Alice. "And ears."

"Yes," said Francis. "Two of them. And eyes."

"And nostrils."

"Absolutely."

"Very ordinary."

"Yes," said Francis. He wanted the next question, he was enjoying himself so much. He even leant forward, as if to catch the question as it came out of Alice's mouth.

"So, Francis," she said. "Where are you from?"

And Francis answered quickly, "Pikipiki."

The name was there in his head, suddenly, big and glowing.

Everybody laughed. This time the laughter surprised Francis—at first.

"There's no such place as Picky-Picky," said Alice.

"Yes," said Francis. "There is."

"No, there isn't," said Alice.

"Yes, there is," said Francis. He had forgotten all about Pikipiki. But it was the first place he'd thought of when Alice asked the question.

"There can't be," said Alice. "It's too mad. What is it again?"

"Pikipiki," said Francis.

He liked saying it again. It was like seeing someone he loved, from far away, coming closer. His father. He had not thought about his father in a long, long time.

"Sir?" said a boy, Liam.

"What?"

"There's no country in Africa called Picky-Picky," said Liam. "I know them all. Morocco, Tunisia, Libya—"

"Thanks, Liam," said Sir. He looked at Francis. "Where's Picky-Picky, Francis?" he asked. "Do you want to talk about it?"

Francis turned to face the teacher. "Yes, sir," he said. "It is where I lived with my father."

"Before you came to Dublin?"

"Yes, sir," said Francis.

"Is it the name of your village?"

"Oh, no, sir," said Francis. "We did not live in a village."

"A city, then," said Sir.

"There's no city in Africa called Picky-Picky, sir," said Liam. "I know them all. There's Alexandria, and—"

"Thanks, Liam," said Sir. "So, Francis. Is it a city?"

"No, sir."

"It's a country?"

"Yes, sir."

Francis heard several children groaning, an oh-no-here-we-go-again kind of groan.

"Bor-ring!"

"Someone else's turn."

"Quiet!" said Sir loudly. He turned back to Francis: "Where, Francis? Where's Picky-Picky?"

Francis put a finger to the side of his head. "In here, sir."

"In your head?"

"Yes, sir," said Francis. "In my head. And in my father's head."

"So it's an imaginary place?"

"No, sir," said Francis. "It is real."

Then they heard Alice.

"Ahem."

Everybody laughed. Francis laughed, too. He turned back to face Alice.

"I *am* supposed to be the interviewer, you know," said Alice. "It *is* a chat show and I do have the biggest mouth in the class. You said that, sir."

"You're right, Alice," said Sir. "You take over from here."

Alice looked at the camera and blinked. "Welcome back," she said. "So, Francis. Tell us a bit about Piggy-Piggy."

"Pikipiki," said Francis.

"Whatever," said Alice. "Tell us all about it."

Francis sat up straight. "My father knew many languages." He stopped. He started again. "My father *knows* many languages," he said.

It was five years since Francis had seen his father.

"One day," he said, "a man passed us by on a motor-bike. And my father told me the word for motorbike in eleven different languages."

"Eleven?"

"Yes," said Francis. "And the one that made me laugh was *pikipiki*."

"So," said Alice. "'Picky-Picky' means 'motorbike'?"

"Yes," said Francis.

"In what language?" asked Alice.

"Swahili," said Francis.

"You're telling us you lived in a country called Motor-bike?"

"Yes," said Francis. "We made it up, my father and I. On the street. My father was—*is*—the king, and I am the prince."

"Prince Francis."

"Yes," said Francis. "When I was with my father—when we were together—we lived in Pikipiki. When he came home from work. When I woke up in the morning. He would say, 'How is the prince of Pikipiki?' It was our country. We had our own money. And our own food. And everything. We made it up."

"Is your father still there?"

Francis nodded.

"Does he phone you?" Alice asked.

Francis shook his head. "My mother says they will not let him phone."

"Who are 'they'?"

"The soldiers," said Francis.

It was five years since Francis and his mother had had to leave their country, in the time of shooting and fires. In those years, since he had come to Dublin, Francis had forgotten much. He had been a little boy when he left. He could not remember everything—it could not be expected. But he remembered, today, Pikipiki, the Kingdom of the Motorbike.

He sat up. He'd remembered something else.

"In Pikipiki," he said, "the mobile phones have wheels."

"Cool," said Alice. "That makes sense."

"Yes," said Francis. "You speak into the phone and put it on the ground. Then it goes very quickly to whoever you are talking to and comes back with the message."

Everybody laughed. They loved the idea of the wheelie mobile phones.

"Well, thank you, Francis," said Alice.

"*Prince* Francis, you mean," said Liam.

"Cool!"

From that day on, everybody called him Prince Francis. And Francis was very pleased, because it meant he was their friend. Every time he heard the word "prince," he thought of his father, the king, and it made him feel that his father was near. Francis was a prince now in his two homes, Pikipiki and Ireland. And his father was very proud of him.

ARTICLE 15

WE ALL HAVE THE RIGHT TO BELONG TO A COUNTRY.

UNCLE MEENA

Ibtisam Barakat

I was the only one who knew that Uncle Meena was returning from America to Ramallah that Sunday. He usually wrote, but three days before, he phoned.

"Noora, I am coming home soon." He spoke playfully, stretching the "soon" until I thought not even a minute was left in it.

"When?" I asked. I was eager to spread the news, but he had a different plan.

"I want my visit to be a surprise to everyone else," he confided. "However, you can expect me this Sunday."

"I won't tell," I promised him.

"And I have new stories," he said enticingly. "Although I require Ramallah tales in exchange for my California ones."

My heart danced with affection at the thought of seeing Uncle Meena. "But these days I only have questions, which have been galloping like wild horses through my mind," I warned him.

"Are these Arabian horses?" He laughed, and I laughed with him. I suddenly realized how much I missed Uncle Meena, and I could see the difference between talking with him on the phone and writing letters. Though I loved my uncle's clever words and the new ideas he always had to share, it was nothing like hearing his wonderful voice, always full of lightness and hope like the spring is full of flowers.

It was one o'clock on Sunday when an orange taxi stopped by our house. I had been watching the street all morning and I knew it was Uncle Meena. My heart pounded, urging me to run out and be the first to greet him, but I wanted to show that I had kept his promise. So I waited until Grandma glanced out of the window and realized who was walking down the steps toward our house. She shook with excitement and surprise.

Her cheers announced the arrival of Uncle Meena to everyone in the neighborhood. Mother ran and flung the kitchen and front doors wide open for all to come in. Boys abandoned their soccer games and raced to our house to greet Uncle Meena. Neighbors, children, and relatives all came to see our beloved visitor and wish him a wonderful stay.

I wasn't the only one with questions for Uncle Meena, I could see. Voices of boys and girls arose from everywhere.

"Is America really far away?"

"Exactly how many miles is it from Ramallah?"

"What is it like to go on a plane?"

"Do you have a lot of money?"

"Can you take us with you when you go back?"

"OK," Uncle Meena said as he grabbed the smallest boy and lifted him into the air. "This is how it feels to be on a plane." He ran across the room making airplane noises, and we flocked after him, wanting our turns. The younger ones jumped up to tackle him.

I was thrilled to see Uncle Meena chased by a swirl of children all so happy to play with him. But in my heart I was most anxious for the time when he and I could be on our own and exchange our stories.

Uncle Meena let the children win, pretending surrender. Then he gave a big grunting noise that made them laugh unstoppably, and wrestled them down to the ground while speaking in exaggerated English.

"What did you say?" everyone asked over and over.

"You've forgotten Arabic, Meena?" Grandma gasped. "I hope you have not forgotten Islam, too."

Uncle Meena smiled with affection, then got up and kissed Grandma's hand, as we all do to show respect for our elders.

"Allah yerda alaik," she praised him. "May Allah be pleased with you."

Later that afternoon, when all was calm again, Uncle Meena asked me if I wanted to go for a walk with him into the center of Ramallah. I jumped for joy. But Grandma protested.

"Noora is no longer a child to be taken everywhere," she said. "She's now a young woman. She has just turned thirteen, remember!"

"I think it's good for both young and grown-up women to see as much as they can of the world. Why don't you come with us?" Uncle Meena said playfully to Grandma.

I was so happy to hear that becoming a woman didn't mean having to stay at home. But Grandma wanted to take the time to prepare Uncle Meena's favorite meal for dinner.

"Just don't be gone for long," she said. "The situation in the city has become very dangerous lately."

"We'll be careful," we assured her.

Uncle Meena and I held hands as we ran up the steps to the street. I was eager to tell him everything I knew that he did not. If he learned of all that had happened, I thought, perhaps he would feel as though he had never left us.

"Grandma is upset because she can no longer pray at al-Aqsa Mosque in Jerusalem," I told him. "The Israeli army now requires a permit for Palestinians crossing between Ramallah and Jerusalem, and very few of us are granted this permit."

"I thought only men younger than thirty-five were barred from crossing. Now even old people can't cross?" Uncle Meena raised his voice in protest and sorrow, and I felt bad that I'd upset him. But he asked me to tell him more.

"Grandma thinks that one prayer at al-Aqsa Mosque is worth a thousand prayers anywhere else. Now she just prays at home. She says al-Aqsa is the home of her heart and that is why she doesn't go to pray at the mosque in Ramallah."

"I understand," Uncle Meena said. "Although I do not pray, I too miss al-Aqsa when I'm in America. It's a magical mosque. I have its picture above my desk. Did you know that the huge golden dome that you can see from any-where in Jerusalem covers the rock from where Prophet Muhammad made his journey to heaven?"

"You mean he flew from the mosque where Grandma likes to pray?"

"Yes, that's what the story says in the Koran. He trav-eled on a winged horse named al-Buraq, which flew as fast as lightning, first from Mecca to Jerusalem, then all the way to heaven and back in one night."

"Wouldn't it be great to have a horse like that, Uncle!"

"Where would you go on it if you had?"

"I'd take Grandma to Jerusalem every day to pray and to shop in the Old City, and come and visit you in California so that I could see where you live. We could walk across the Golden Gate Bridge—you sent me a postcard of it last year, right?—and I would ask you all my questions."

"What questions do you have?"

"Do you really want to hear them?"

"Of course I do."

"OK, Uncle. This is my biggest question. Everyone tells me that there is one God. But how come there are many religions that fight against each other, destroying what God creates—like people and olive trees? It takes years for a person or a tree to grow up, and then someone with a gun kills them in a second."

"I don't have any answers, Noora, but I can tell you what I think. For me, God is a magical destination, like a divine city that turns away no one, that people travel to along an endless number of roads. The different faiths and beliefs are the roads. But sometimes people fight because they think that their road, or their idea about this destination, is the only true one."

"How do you know, Uncle?"

"I have friends from many faiths: Muslims, Christians, Hindus, pagans, and also some Jews who care about Palestinians and want the occupation to end. My Native

American friends believe that a wonderful big spirit connects all people, animals, trees, and every living thing in one family of life."

"I feel like this, too! Especially with flowers and trees. Please, Uncle, who are the Native Americans?"

"They are the people who lived in North America before the Europeans came. The clashes between the two groups were extremely violent. The Native Americans, who were also called Indians, suffered great losses. I've been meaning to tell you about one Native American in particular, who is very special to me."

Uncle Meena's voice had changed, as though his heart had spread its wings with happiness.

"A woman?" I guessed.

"Yes!" He nodded.

"Tell me *everything*!"

"But this, too, must be held in confidence, just until I find the right time to tell Mother and everyone else. Yes?"

"Of course!"

He took a moment, filled with smiles, then spoke quietly.

"She is my girlfriend and I love her very much."

I was so pleased for Uncle Meena and knew that wonderful stories would follow. Now I had even more questions! But before I could ask them I realized that, without noticing, Uncle Meena and I were almost at the center of Ramallah and were approaching a spot in the road where a tile had been laid. Everyone was walking around the tile and then carrying on their way. Uncle Meena asked me what the tile signified and I explained that at times, when a Palestinian was killed in a confrontation with the Israeli army, people placed a tile on the spot where the person died. In this symbolic way, those who died in the struggle for our freedom continued to be part of our daily lives.

Uncle Meena gazed at the tile before us. It had no name, no date, and was as anonymous as a raindrop. His tears fell quietly.

As we approached al-Manara Circle, we discovered that we couldn't walk any farther. Tires blazed; flames and smoke danced around the edges of al-Manara like banners of danger. We heard that a military operation in Ramallah was taking place in response to an explosion in Jerusalem.

Uncle Meena and I turned around. As we hurried back, we held hands, but now we were silent and in our separate worlds. I felt that my words and all of my questions had fallen out of my mind and were lost on the streets, like coins that fall out of a pocket and are never found.

Violence raged in Ramallah in the days that followed, and Uncle Meena stayed at home with us. We were content to be with him, although often he didn't speak. For hours his face was as empty as a bus station with no passengers waiting.

"Leave him alone," Grandma would say. "He is in California."

If he were in California, I thought, his face would be happy, just like when he had spoken of his Native American girlfriend there. "I think he is in Jerusalem, Grandma, visiting al-Aqsa Mosque with you," I wanted to say. I wanted to tell her how sad he had felt when he'd learned she could no longer cross the checkpoint to pray at al-Aqsa. But I was certain that would make her cry with longing.

One day, Uncle Meena heard some children in the yard shouting and fighting. He went outside to investigate, and Grandma and I joined him. The children were playing Jews and Arabs. They were wrestling and pretending to fight.

"In America we call this game Cowboys and Indians— but in America you would all be Indians," said Uncle Meena.

"We're not Indians!" they all protested.

"I'm an Indian, too, and so is Grandma and everyone in Ramallah," he continued. "Red Indians. And those soldiers are the cowboys."

"Don't confuse the children, Meena," Grandma chided.

"They're already confused. War is confusing." He began to cry.

Now the children stood staring at him and at one another. They didn't know what to do. I pointed to a soccer ball in the field and they all raced toward it, ending the Cowboys-and-Indians game. Grandma looked at the ground to conceal her tears, and Uncle Meena went to his room. I wished I knew what I could do to help him. I wanted to understand. Later I knocked gently on his door.

"Come in!" he called.

"Why do you say we're all Indians, Uncle?" I whispered, walking in hesitantly.

"Because our people's story is the story of the Indians." He hugged me. "The tile of America has the broken freedom of the Indians under it. We are the Indians of Palestine."

His talk of America brought to my mind the only American I had ever met.

It was in our village outside Ramallah, when I was visiting some of my relatives. He was a tourist whose car had broken down. He shrieked for help, and quickly everyone in the village gathered around him. Pointing to his chest, he said, "American." We felt as though we had won a prize. An American in our midst!

A group of men took him to the *madafeh,* the village guest house, while other men fixed his car. The women cooked for him. He offered money. We raised our eyebrows in surprise; he offered more. We laughed and gestured no. We tried to explain that Arabs feed their guests before they feed themselves, that we love a guest anytime. Finally he understood.

The American was the talk of the village for days. Many women thought him beautiful. They wished they had blue eyes like his, even if just for a day. They wanted to know what it was like to see the world with different-colored eyes. Now I thought that perhaps it was like having a different faith.

After supper that night Uncle Meena wanted to go up on the roof and gaze at the star-freckled face of the sky till we fell asleep. Despite Grandma's warnings I snatched the thin flashlight from the kitchen drawer, and he and I went up and lay on our backs in the dark. Mother and Grandma soon followed us, carrying pillows.

"Tell us about California. Do you love it?" Mom asked Uncle Meena.

"Very much," he said.

Suddenly everything in me became fully awake, as though the story I was about to hear were the morning sun. I knew that now was the moment when Uncle Meena would tell Mom and Grandma about his girlfriend, and I wanted to hear every word.

Uncle Meena reached for his wallet and pulled out a tiny photo. He handed it to me. "This is Panu," he said.

I turned on my side and held the photograph, shining the light on it. Panu's hair was dark like the night that surrounded us. Her eyes were dark also. She smiled out at me; I smiled back.

Mother and Grandma wanted to see the photo too. "Is she Indian?" they asked.

"Yes," Uncle Meena replied. "Like you and me."

We all laughed.

"If that be God's will, I accept it," Grandma said with a sigh.

"Panu let me into her world like an Arab lets a stranger stay in his home for three days before asking him what he wants," Uncle Meena said. "She took me to what is referred to in America as a reservation. The Rez, she called it."

"What do they reserve there, Uncle?" I asked.

"People," he said. "It's like a Palestinian refugee camp."

I was shocked to hear there were reservations in America. I had thought that everyone in the world was free except for the Palestinians. But I was also excited to learn a new English word and couldn't wait to tell my friends that al-Am'ari Refugee Camp, at the edge of Ramallah, was like a Native American reservation. Now I understood why Uncle Meena said we were all Indians.

"Panu and I met at the university. I chose to study history; she chose linguistics, as she wants to create records, perhaps dictionaries, of dying American Indian languages.

One day she pulled off her shelf a dictionary of a language called Miwok. 'Who are the Miwok?' I asked. 'I will tell you tomorrow,' she said.

"The next morning, she drove me to a glorious mountain called Tamalpais, which rises up from the shore and touches the clouds. We sat facing the water. 'The Miwok tribe lived on this mountain,' she said. 'I come here to see the ocean through their eyes. I hear their voices calling in the wind like prayers. This place is my temple.'

"'What happened to the Miwok?' I asked. She told me that most of them had disappeared. In 1851, only two hundred and fifty were left; in 1880, the number had gone down to sixty. In 1920, they became five, and then in 1930, there were—"

But we did not hear any more numbers, because Grandma screamed for Uncle Meena to stop. She didn't want to hear him say that none remained.

"Mother," he continued, "the Miwok were only one tribe of hundreds of American Indian tribes that lost all or most of their people. But many also survived."

Now Grandma snatched up Panu's photograph and brought it close to her face as though Panu were her daughter. She gasped with grief.

"Did you give her a ring, Meena?" she asked.

"Yes." Uncle Meena spoke timidly, as he hadn't consulted Grandma first. But he no longer needed to.

Grandma had taken Panu into her heart through Uncle Meena's story.

"Panu only wanted my word—and for a ring, a dandelion from the highest peak of Mount Tamalpais to wrap around her finger. She said that when asked if it would give its spirit in the celebration of love, the flower would say yes. Panu told me that I would hear in my heart the answer of the flower."

Suddenly I felt I had no more questions that night. A sense of peace filled me. The stars above became sky dandelions that grew in the heavens, searching for a girl's finger. And our eyes became those of our people who had gone before us and seen the same sky and prayed to God for wishes only their hearts knew, and the eyes of those who would come after us and pray for new wishes.

Cool night breeze tickled our toes and persuaded us to retreat. But before we did, Uncle Meena told us that he must return to California. He and I would have to go back to communicating through letters and postcards.

The next day, he departed as he had arrived, quickly, tears filling his eyes and Grandma's. He carried an extra sack that Grandma had filled with sage, thyme, dried okra, pickled *labaneh* yogurt and roasted wheat, and roasted chickpeas for Panu. I slipped in a note with a greeting on it: *With love for Panu—from the Indians of Palestine.*

And I was left dreaming of the piercing smile of a Native

American girl. Someday she would come to Ramallah, and I would have many questions for her. Or perhaps someday, if I asked with all my heart, I would have a winged horse that could gallop at the speed of light. I would cross the ocean at sunrise to sit with Panu and Uncle Meena on top of Mount Tamalpais and look out over the water. We would each pray in our own way, and fill the ocean with prayers that all people be free.

ARTICLE 18

WE ALL HAVE THE RIGHT TO BELIEVE IN WHAT WE WANT TO BELIEVE. WE HAVE THE RIGHT TO HAVE A RELIGION AND TO CHANGE IT IF WE WANT.

SEARCHING FOR
A TWO-WAY STREET

Malorie Blackman

Before I was born,
Grown-ups were passports
And driving licences
And bank accounts
And utility bills.

Communication was
Mobile phones
And cyber chats
And sign language
And face-to-face.

But people were
"Hello"

And hugs
And "Pleased to meet you"
And "How are you?"

Songs were
"Talk to me,"
"See my side,"
"Be with me,"
"Love me."

And all those things
Were proof
Of a person's identity.

All those things
Said
"I'm here,
I'm now,
I'm ready,
Willing,
And able
To communicate."
But that was
Before I was born.

Before I was born,

There weren't cameras
And scanners
And microchip readers
On every roof
On every street corner.

Before I was born,
School wasn't just a screen
And a virtual teacher.
Friends across the world
Had real faces,
Not faces chosen
In games or
From a menu.
We were more
Than just serial numbers
And chips with everything.

Before I was born,
There was such a thing as
Secrecy
Mystery
Privacy.
Before I was born.

Not anymore.

When I was born,
A microchip was implanted
At the base of my skull.
No microchip?
No state benefits,
No health care,
No travel,
No food aid,
No water deliveries,
No shelter,
No existence.
No microchip equals
no anything.
Nothing.
No thing.
Not a thing.
So my mum and dad
Agreed,
When I was born,
To my microchip
Implant.
"We want our son
To survive in this world.
So yes to the chip."
Mum and Dad didn't like it,
They didn't want it,

But they had no choice.
And the government now knows
Where I am at all times.
Where any of us
Each of us
Are
At all times.
And we let them
Do that to us.

The government said,
"Law-abiding citizens
Have nothing to fear."

The government said,
"Those with nothing to hide
Have nothing to fear.

"The curtailment
Of a personal freedom
Or two
Is a small price to pay
If we wish to have
Nothing to fear,"
The government said.

Those were the reasons
We gave up our mystery.

Better not to question.
Better not to know.
Better to accept.

And our information is fed
Back to computers.
State-of-the-art recording devices
That sit in silence
And capture all movements
All meetings
All positions.

And Mum told me,
"Thirty years ago
This would've been
Inconceivable."

And Dad said,
"Twenty years ago
This would've been
Unthinkable."

"Information shouldn't be

A one-way street," said Mum.
"Who watches the Watchmen?"
Said Dad.

But they whisper the words
Behind closed doors.
It doesn't pay
To stand and say
How you feel.
Not yesterday.
Not today.
Not tomorrow.
"Those days are over,"
Mum and Dad sigh.

There's a rumour
Going round.
True or not?
Who can say?
But I think . . . true.
And this rumour?
The microchips in our heads
At the base of our brains
Relay our thinking;
Maybe even control
Our thinking.

Just a rumour
But it's smoke . . .
So where's the fire?
Inside
Or outside
Our heads?

There's a rumour
Going round
That
Full thoughts
Whole sentences
Can be tracked
Traced
Monitored.
So I try
To think
In short
Sharp
Bursts.
My best friend
Denny told me
Staccato thoughts
Come across
Like static
White noise.

No rhyme
No reason.
No sense
Nonsense.
True or not?
Who can say?

But now I think
In bursts
Like bullets
Fired from a gun.
Proper sentences
Could make me
. . . disappear.

Thoughts ought to be private,
Information ought to be shared,
Communication should be
A two-way street.
An optional road to travel.
But a road we all
Can take
Nonetheless.

"Those days
Are over,"

Mum and Dad murmur.
But I'm not prepared
To believe that.
There has to be a way,
Some way,
To make my life
My own again.
Some way.

So I've started looking
For a means,
Some manner
To make my life
A two-way street.
And I will find it,
Because I'm not alone
In thinking
In bursts
Like bullets
Fired from a gun.
I'm not alone.
Because you are here
Sharing these thoughts.
And I hope
You think the same.
Feel the same.

Our two-way street
We shall find
We shall explore
We shall travel
Together.

ARTICLE 19

WE ALL HAVE THE RIGHT TO MAKE UP OUR OWN
MINDS, TO THINK WHAT WE LIKE, TO SAY WHAT
WE THINK, AND TO SHARE OUR IDEAS WITH OTHER
PEOPLE, WHEREVER THEY LIVE, THROUGH BOOKS,
RADIO, TELEVISION, AND IN OTHER WAYS.

SETTING WORDS FREE

Margaret Mahy

DANIEL'S sister, Diana, was watering the garden; the hose undulated behind her like a thin green snake.

A snake! Of course, thought Daniel.

Water shot out in front of Diana in a curve of silver snake spit, pattering down onto the cabbage leaves.

"Hey!" she called. "Your turn now. You can water the mustard and cress."

"No, I can't," said Daniel. "I've got ophidiophobia." He grinned. First time of using! He'd never thought he'd find a chance to use *that* word. He punched the air above his head.

Diana groaned in exasperation. "No, you *haven't,*" she yelled, and then her face brightened. "Dad! Dad! He's doing it again."

Daniel had not heard his father come up behind them.

"What's he doing again?" asked their father.

"He's using stupid words," Diana complained. "Not swear words. Just stupid ones. Those he gets from that book with the blue cover. And he won't take a turn at watering."

"I just said I had ophidiophobia," said Daniel defensively. "That means 'fear of snakes'—a dread of snakes. The hose scares me."

"No, it doesn't," said his father. He took the hose from Diana and thrust it at Daniel, who took it reluctantly. "I wish you'd forget this obsession with words and join the Olympic Sports Club. Play rugby, like I did when I was your age. It's great fun."

"I don't want to play rugby," said Daniel, turning the snake spit onto the mustard and cress. "Well, I don't want to play it *seriously*. I'm a word boy. I want to use all the words in the world."

"There's no point in using words no one else can understand," argued Diana.

"It's good for a boy to have a lively vocabulary," said their mother, arriving to see what they were quarrelling about.

"Too true," agreed his father, "and I don't care if he *does* use all the words in the world. But he needs a bit of balance. Whoa, be careful, Daniel. You're supposed to be watering those plants, not drowning them!"

Daniel sighed. Years ago his father had been captain of a rugby team, and it had been a glorious time for him. These days he wanted to relive his memories by seeing Daniel follow in his footsteps. But though Daniel liked watching rugby, he didn't want to be part of that tumbling world.

"You never know, you might find another word boy at the Olympic Sports Club," his father went on, grinning. "You certainly hear a lot of interesting words spinning around in a scrum."

Daniel laughed. "You and Mum wouldn't want me to use words like those!"

Oddly enough, the very next day he *did* hear some words that caught his attention.

He was on his way home from school, more or less keeping pace with a group of shouting kids wearing the blue uniform of Marley Street College, a run-down school streets away from his own. A whole hive of words buzzed around him as the kids yelled to one another, but they were all words Daniel already knew.

"You talk a load of rubbish," shouted a voice right behind Daniel, but it wasn't talking to him.

"Oi! Excuse me! When I use a word, it means what

I *tell* it to mean," a second voice — a husky voice — shouted back. "Neither more nor less," it added. Then it laughed to itself.

Daniel knew that his father had once lived in the Marley Street part of town, and had worked hard to leave it — along with that blue school uniform — far behind. His father was proud of the fact that these days he drove a smart car and lived in a house with a beautiful view. It was almost as if he had crossed over into a different country.

"You can't tell words what to mean," said the first voice, sounding scornful.

"Yes, I can. Yes, I do," said the second voice. "I'm a word boss."

Both voices were the voices of girls, but Daniel couldn't have said which of the twisting gang of kids behind him had spoken. All the same, because he was secretly fascinated by words and the games that could be played with them, he shot a glance back over his shoulder.

"Hey! What are *you* staring at?" one girl yelled at him.

"You boys from St. Catherine's are always trying to feel us up," said another, and the kids around her burst out laughing.

Daniel knew that any clever reply would bring yet another wave of derision crashing over him. This was one of those times when it was sensible to be a word coward.

He turned his back on them, ignoring their Marley Street jeers. They sang their mocking chorus:

"St. Cat's! St. Cat's!
They're a bunch of stuck-up brats!"

"On the way home from school I heard someone saying that they *tell* their words what to mean," Daniel told his parents at dinner that evening.

"Sounds like someone who enjoys reading," his father said. "That comes from one of the Alice books, doesn't it? *Alice's Adventures in Wonderland*, maybe. Lewis Carroll, anyway!"

"Humpty Dumpty said it," his mother declared. "The Humpty Dumpty in *Through the Looking-Glass*, that is. "'When *I* use a word, it means just what I choose it to mean — neither more nor less.'"

Daniel's mother knew her books.

"That's just what this girl said!" Daniel exclaimed.

"You overhear things like that when you go to a good school," his father said.

Daniel did not tell him that he had been listening to a girl from Marley Street. Marley Street was like a different country, and the school he went to cost his parents a great deal of money.

But the next day, Daniel chose, once again, to go the

long way home. And, once again, he found himself caught up in the middle of a group of Marley Street pupils. He glanced sideways at them, thinking that they seemed to be more of a mixture than the kids at his school. Some of them didn't seem very different from him, but a lot of them looked scruffy, as if their uniforms did not fit properly.

"It's against the law," one of them now cried out.

"Laws! Laws are inherited like diseases," someone else answered in a showing-off way.

There it was again—that girl's husky voice. Had she actually made that up? Daniel stepped to one side and paused so he could watch her walk by. This time he could pick her out. She was a tall, thin girl, her face spattered with freckles, her hair standing out around her head like a rusting halo.

"Law or not, a fool and his money are soon partying," Daniel quickly said, adapting a phrase he had found in his blue quotations book.

Almost nobody noticed him. But the tall girl with the rusty hair turned and stared at him. It was as if he had spoken a password she had recognized. She took half a step towards him, and then stopped.

"You didn't make that up," she said.

There they stood, staring challengingly at each other, while the rest of the noisy group twisted on ahead of them.

"You don't make things up either," Daniel retorted. "But when it comes to your crowd, you should develop lipostomy," he added quickly.

"What?" she asked, and he could tell she was not only taken aback, but also curious. That word had been like bait, and she was hooked.

He took a breath, anxious to explain that "lipostomy" was a condition of the mouth that prevented people from speaking.

But then someone grabbed the girl's arm, shouting something to her, and she let herself be dragged away, looking back at Daniel once and then probably forgetting him and his odd word altogether.

The next day was Saturday. Daniel wandered out of his gate—an elegant wrought-iron gate—and found himself looking across the big park. Marley Street was on the other side, and somewhere in the Marley Street suburb was that disreputable school. And somewhere over there, talking her way through the world, was that freckled girl who played jokes with quotations and was curious about words. He walked to and fro in a shuffling way, trying to trick himself into feeling careless. If by some chance he found himself strolling off across the park, he wanted it to feel like an accident.

"Where are you going?" asked Diana, suddenly

appearing behind him. She was younger than he was, but she often tried to tag along.

"None of your business," said Daniel. "Anyway, I'm not going anywhere much."

But once she had gone back inside, he set off quickly down the street and jogged through a small grove of oak trees and out into the great open space beyond. Grassy land rose and fell before him like the waves of a strange sea, wrinkling, but frozen in the middle of its wrinkling. Up, over, and on! Up, over, and on! Joggers puffed past him. A father with three little children played a game with a red ball.

Every now and then Daniel turned round, glancing behind him, half feeling he was being followed; but no one he could see in the softly surging parkland looked like any sort of spy. Unless, of course, there was someone hiding in the bushes that ran around the boundary. Certain leaves seemed to be quivering with something more than a mere summer breeze. Ahead of him the park ended with hedges, wooden palings, and an arched gateway at the top of a small flight of steps. Intrigued by this boundary into another land, Daniel strolled on.

As he approached that faraway edge, the park seemed to deteriorate around him. The grass dried up as if it had not been watered in the same careful way that *his* end of the park had been. There was a children's playground off to the left, but the seesaw was snapped in half and one of the swings hung crookedly. There was something desolate about that dangling swing, quivering just a little in the slight wind, its broken chain snaking in the muddy puddle under the seat.

"Just as well I've got over my ophidiophobia," Daniel told it, laughing to himself. "You can't scare me."

Climbing the steps, he reached the arched gateway, walked boldly through it, and found himself confronting a street of small, crowded houses hunched shoulder to shoulder as if they were defending themselves from some hovering blow—some city council plan to have them all demolished and replaced with modern apartments, perhaps. One house had a window, broken and boarded over, which made it look as if it were a pirate house, staring across the ocean of grass from a single damaged eye.

Daniel could see a jumble of buildings farther down the street, which stood out against the skyline, green against blue. The school. *Marley Street* said a sign on a telegraph pole, and just beyond that was a pedestrian crossing with a notice reminding motorists to slow down. Daniel wandered over to the gates. A school shed with its back to the street was covered with graffiti—well-known four-letter words, easy to spell but forbidden to say. However, the school walls themselves were clean enough. Off to the right, rugby goalposts stretched up, staring at each other across an empty pitch.

"Hi!" came a voice from behind him.

Daniel turned and, amazingly, there she was, her rusty hair burning with sunlight, her freckles like specks of gold. Now that she was standing in front of him, Daniel allowed himself to admit that he had been hoping to bump into her all along. Some lucky accident had brought them face-to-face on a Saturday, free from their school uniforms, her noisy schoolmates, and their different countries.

"What are *you* doing here?" she asked derisively.

"I'm allowed to be here if I want," Daniel replied. "It's a free country. That space back there, that's a free park."

"You're from that posh school," she said. "The stuck-up one! And you were hanging around us yesterday. You come from over *there,* don't you?" she went on, pointing.

Daniel looked back across the park and found he could actually make out the sharp roof of the tall house that was his home.

"You live where rich people live. But where wealth accumulates, men decay."

She looked at him intently as she said this, to see if he recognized it. Daniel grinned.

"How come you say things like that?" he asked. "I heard you doing it the other day, too."

She shrugged. "Me? I just make things up."

"No, you don't. You get them from books. The other day you were quoting Humpty Dumpty."

"Humpty Dumpty!" she exclaimed indignantly. "No, I wasn't."

"Yes, you were. Humpty Dumpty from *Through the Looking-Glass,*" Daniel explained. "It's a book."

"Oh, *that* Humpty Dumpty," she said. "I know it's a book. I've read it. I can read, you know," she added, looking at him with a dark, gingery expression.

"What are you reading now?" asked Daniel. He felt his question was somehow silly, yet at the same time he wanted to know.

The girl stared at him. *"Oliver Twist,"* she said. "It's really good."

As they talked, they had been edging forward side by side. Now they reached the small flight of steps that led down into the park.

"*Oliver Twist*? That's a classic," said Daniel, making way for her.

"Have *you* read it?" she asked over her shoulder.

"Not really," he admitted reluctantly, wishing he could say that he had. "We've got a copy of it at home, though."

"The one I'm reading is sort of shortened," she said. "My dad says a shortened book doesn't count, but I think it counts a bit. Anyway, I'm really enjoying it. What are you reading?"

"The last Harry Potter," he said. "I've read it once, and now I'm reading it again."

"Harry Potter's OK," said the girl, rather patronizingly. "'Please, sir, I want some more.'" She grinned at Daniel. He had the idea she was quoting something yet again. "Bits of books work their way into my head, and come out when I talk," she said.

A bush at the edge of the park quivered once more.

"I've got to go," said Daniel, looking at his watch. He hesitated. "What's your name?"

"Tessie," she said. "Tessie Markham. What's yours?"

"Daniel," he said. "Daniel Harrison. See you around!"

"Maybe!" Tessie answered, turning in the opposite direction. "Maybe not, though."

That evening, Daniel could tell his father was annoyed about something.

"I hear you've been hanging around Marley Street," he said eventually.

Daniel looked at him, startled.

"No use trying to have any secrets from me," his father said. "How did you wind up over there?"

Daniel shrugged. "I just walked across the park," he said. He noticed Diana staring down at her bowl of vegetable soup as if she expected to read her fortune there among the onion and carrots. He remembered the twitching bushes. Typical! She must have followed him and seen him meeting Tessie. And then she had raced home to tell tales.

"Probably a good thing to keep away from that part of town," his father went on. "It's not safe. Gangs hang out there. You could get beaten up."

"Not in the afternoon," argued Daniel. "Anyhow, that girl I was talking to—she isn't in a gang. She reads a lot. *Alice in Wonderland* and *Oliver Twist*. Good books like that. And she pointed over here, at St. Catherine's, and said that when men accumulate a lot of wealth, they decay."

His father's expression changed. One moment he was annoyed. The next he was interested without quite meaning to be.

"She didn't make that up," he said. "'Where wealth accumulates and men decay . . .' I don't know who said it first, but it certainly wasn't her."

"Maybe she learnt it at school," Daniel suggested.

His father's face hardened again.

"Listen, Daniel!" he said. "That part of town has always been shifty. I should know—I lived there once, but I got away from it all. I want you to keep clear of it. And I don't want you winding up with a Marley Street girlfriend either."

"Girls don't play rugby," said Diana cheekily. She was enjoying Daniel's discomfort and did not want it to stop.

"I'm allowed to have friends who read," Daniel argued. "I've got a right to choose my own friends, despite . . ." He struggled to put his thought into words. "I mean, just because someone's from a different . . ." He broke off and began again. "What's wrong with having friends who fit in with me?"

"Nothing," his father began. "But . . ." Then he stopped. "Listen, Dan, it's my job to look after you for a few more years," he said at last. "And I don't want you hanging around Marley Street. Right?"

"She could come over here," suggested Diana slyly.

"No, she couldn't!" their father exclaimed. "Next thing we know, we'd have the walls of our house sprayed with filthy words and thugs thumping all over our garden."

And both Diana and Daniel fell silent.

"You should have boys for friends," Diana said later. "Join that Olympic Sports Club like Dad wants you to."

"Dad's always on at me to hang out with rugby boys," Daniel complained. "I like to *watch* rugby, but I don't much want to *play* it just because Dad used to. I like playing tennis. And when that girl—Tessie—says something, then I say something back. It's sort of like playing *word* tennis."

And, in the days that followed, Daniel and Tessie went on meeting in a curious, half-secret way. It depended who was around. Sometimes they walked home after school on opposite sides of the street, exchanging glances. Sometimes they were both late leaving school, perhaps on purpose, and felt able to walk together. They always tried to bring surprising sayings with them.

"'The first duty of a revolutionary is to get away with it,'" said Tessie.

"Where did you read that?" Daniel asked.

"It doesn't matter," she said. "The thing is—well, right now it isn't just shut up in some book. Me, I like to set words flying out into the open air like paper aeroplanes." She laughed, waving her arms above her head as if she were indeed turning words loose. "It's a sort of law that words should be free," she said, still laughing, but more to herself.

"'Laws are inherited like diseases,'" Daniel responded.

Tessie stopped and stared at him. "Where did you read *that*?" she asked.

"It doesn't matter," Daniel retorted smugly. He waved his arms, too, and they both laughed.

Over the next few weeks they continued to meet, and paddled along the edge of that grassy sea separating their different countries—Daniel's country and Tessie's—gossiping, arguing, and setting words free as they talked. They did not meet every day, but often enough for Daniel to feel that the whole park had come alive with the strange words they turned loose, sometimes fluttering, sometimes stinging. He felt that he and Tessie were playing a secret language game . . . building a bridge that crossed the grassy sea, tying one side of the park to the other.

"Do you think what we've got is eccentricity?" Daniel asked one day, hoping to trick her into asking what it meant.

"Who cares? It isn't catching!" Tessie replied, and added triumphantly, "Eccentricity is an outlaw."

Sometimes Daniel's father would tackle him about this strange friendship, frowning to himself as if he were working out a riddle with an answer that kept slipping away.

"But, Dad, look—I've a right to have a good friend, haven't I?" Daniel said over and over again.

Daniel's mum took his side.

"All they do is wander around talking," she reasoned. "No harm in that. And anyhow, you've had some funny friends too. What about Tommy Bartlett?"

"Tommy?" said Mr. Harrison. His face softened. "Well, he was a real character. I mean—OK, he was rough as a sack—but he always made me laugh."

"Did he make jokes?" Daniel asked. "Jokes with words?"

"He was full of jokes," his father replied. "There's no one I know these days who makes me laugh the way Tommy used to."

One day Daniel arrived home late, full of fear that his father might pick up on his lateness and might actually forbid him to cross the grassy ocean to Tessie's country ever again. But, though it was dinnertime, his father was not home yet.

"I'll keep it warm for him," said Daniel's mother, sliding a full plate into the oven.

"You should let him get his own dinner," said Diana. "Lots of dads cook these days."

"Oh, I know," said their mother, "but your dad's working hard at the moment. I don't think it's much fun for him, so he deserves a bit of spoiling when he comes home. He'll be worn out."

But when their father did come home, he did not look tired. He burst in on them with a huge grin, dropped his briefcase, and flung his arms wide.

"Hello, my wonderful ones!" he cried.

Their mother's expression changed. "You've been *drinking*!" she declared.

The children watched as their father slumped into an armchair, still smiling, but heaving a great sigh at the same time.

"Too true," he said, "but I didn't drink much; I promise I didn't. Just enough to make me feel rather . . . I don't know . . . jolly. Lighthearted! I met up with Tommy Bartlett and—"

"Tommy Bartlett!" their mother said thoughtfully. "He's, er, out of jail, then?"

Their father twisted his head from side to side as if he were trying to stop her words from wriggling into his ears.

"I know, I know," he said. "But he still makes me laugh. It was a sort of relief to be in his company again, just for a little while."

Mrs. Harrison said nothing, but her husband must have read something in her face.

"Look, I have the right to choose my own friends, and—"

But then he stopped—stopped in the middle of his sentence. He looked sideways at Daniel. "I *do* have the right to have friends that fit in with me," he said slowly. "Even if they come from some other country."

"What country does Tommy Bartlett come from?" asked Daniel.

His father leant forward and buried his face in his hands. He groaned softly.

"Marley Street," he mumbled. "Marley Street!" He lifted his head. "And he's been in jail for hitting a policeman. Look! I broke free from Marley Street, emigrated to another land. I don't want you sliding back in *that* direction." He sighed and thumped the arm of the chair. "But, all right, I suppose you do have the right to choose your friends. As long as they're *good* friends, I don't suppose it matters too much what country they come from."

"He hates to be reminded of his Marley Street time," said Daniel's mother later, when she came in to say good night to Daniel. "But he can't quite turn his back on Tommy Bartlett. Anyhow, it sounds as if he's ready to let you and your friend Tessie build your word castles after all."

"We don't build castles," Daniel said. "We just read books, say the words, and let them fly around free."

"Good on you! Most words should be free," agreed his mother. "Not all of them, of course," she added quickly, "just most of them. But do invite her here sometime, and I'll stop faffing about and think of some good words myself. Now, night-night!"

She moved towards the door.

"Hey," shouted Daniel. "What does 'faffing about' mean?"

His mother laughed. "Look it up, word boy!" she said as she switched off the light. "Or work it out for yourself."

And she left him there, his head lying calmly on the cool pillow but spinning inside with the surprise of life and the thrill of words that jostled and danced freely—no matter which country you happened to live in.

ARTICLE 20

WE ALL HAVE THE RIGHT TO MEET OUR FRIENDS
AND TO WORK TOGETHER IN PEACE TO DEFEND
OUR RIGHTS. NOBODY CAN MAKE US JOIN A GROUP
IF WE DON'T WANT TO.

JOJO LEARNS TO DANCE

Meja Mwangi

JOJO knew that something out of the ordinary was about to happen the moment he saw Popo the Wise arrive. Slowly and thoughtfully Popo sat down in the shade under a tree to wait. Then others came in small groups, talking excitedly among themselves. The largest group brought with them a huge wooden box, which they placed in the corner of the yard. They began hopping on one foot, singing, "Zozo! Zozo! Zozo!"

Jojo had never seen anything like it.

"Zozo," his mother explained. "It's all about Zozo."

"*Uncle* Zozo?" Jojo asked. "What's happened to him?"

"Nothing," she said. "Now, run to Aunt Gogo's house and tell her I need her help."

By the time Jojo returned, his mother's yard resembled a marketplace. There were visitors everywhere, and more were arriving every minute. Jojo was more than a little worried. His mother was busy, so he went in search of someone who could tell him what Uncle Zozo had done to cause such chaos.

"No, Zozo is not dead," Uncle Dodo said to him. "Zozo is coming."

Uncle Zozo had visited before, but never had there been so many to receive him.

"This is different," said Uncle Dodo. "Zozo is going to be the big one."

Uncle Zozo was bigger and stronger than anyone Jojo knew.

"He's going to be a leader," Uncle Dodo explained. "In Parliament. We are here to give him our support."

Jojo went away somewhat reassured, but still confused. He would have liked to ask more questions but was afraid of being thought foolish.

"You are too young to understand!" was what they usually said to him. Jojo had heard this all his life. But how would he ever learn anything if he was always considered too young to understand?

"I'll tell you what you want to know," said his cousin Lolo. "Ask me anything."

"Where is Parliament?"

"Parliament?" she said. "I don't know."

"And why is Uncle Zozo going there?" Jojo asked her.

"I don't know," she said again. "Ask me something simpler."

"You don't know anything," he said crossly.

"I know why Uncle Zozo is coming."

"So do I."

Just then a loud cry rose from the crowd, drowning out everything else. Uncle Zozo had arrived in a huge car accompanied by hordes of dancers carrying placards and yelling, "Zozo! Zozo! Zozo!" The crowd gave way for the car, going wild when Uncle Zozo finally stepped out. He looked magnificent.

The cheers became louder when he climbed onto the wooden box, raised his arms in the air, and began to shout, "Vote for . . ."

"Zozo!"

"Vote for . . ."

"Zozo!"

The crowd clapped and danced and waved their placards. Some cut branches from overhanging trees and shook them above their heads.

"Vote for Zozo!" they sang. "Vote for Zozo!"

Uncle Zozo silenced them with a wave. "You all know

me," he said to them. "I look like you, talk like you, fly like you, and think like you. I'm one of you. No one cares more about your welfare than I do. I'm a crow!"

"Zozo!" the crowd chanted. "Zozo!"

"You will never regret sending me to represent you," Uncle Zozo continued. "I promise you that if you vote for me, I will never sleep again."

There was more that Jojo wanted to ask, but Cousin Lolo had left his side in the commotion following Uncle Zozo's arrival. Popo the Wise stood a short distance away, keenly watching the proceedings.

Popo was the oldest crow in Crow Town. Everyone went to Popo when they were troubled or did not know what else to do. Otherwise they left him well alone to think his wise thoughts. Children were instructed never to bother him when he was thinking. Jojo knew this, but his unanswered question still bothered him.

"Grandfather?" he asked, approaching him. "Where is Parliament?"

"Parliament?" Popo the Wise said absently.

"Where Uncle Zozo's going."

"Only if we let him," Popo said, shaking his head.

"You will never be sorry if you elect me," Uncle Zozo could be heard to say from his box. "You will have the best schools, the best hospitals, roads, houses—you name it."

"Jobs?" someone asked.

"The best jobs," agreed Uncle Zozo.

"Money?" asked another.

"That too."

"I don't know," Popo the Wise said to Jojo. "I acknowledge that he's a crow like us, but I'd think very hard before electing anyone who promises so much. Sorry—what was it you wanted to know?"

"Parliament," Jojo reminded him. "Where is it?"

"You don't know where Parliament is?" Popo seemed surprised.

"No one takes me anywhere," Jojo grumbled. "I'm too young to do anything."

"Nonsense," said Popo the Wise. "No one is too young to learn. When I was your age I flew to the sea by myself. I'm too old to do that now, but I can still teach you a thing or two."

"*Everything?*" Jojo asked.

"I'll tell you what I can," said Popo.

Jojo could hardly contain himself. "Popo!" He hopped with excitement. "Popo! Popo!"

Popo the Wise placed his wing on his grandson's shoulder to quiet him. They turned back to listen to Zozo again.

"Some of you crows prefer to fly with the eagles," Uncle Zozo was saying to the crowd. "You promise your support but then vote for others instead. I'll not stand

161

for it. I expect each and every one of you to vote for me. Remember, I'm watching you. Vote for . . ."

"Zozo!"

"Vote for . . ."

"Zozo!"

The crowd danced wildly, waving their placards and their branches. Forgetting that he wasn't supposed to ask any more questions, Jojo tugged on Popo's sleeve. "What does he mean, 'vote'?"

"Choose," said Popo. "'Vote' means choose."

"Choose what?"

"Choose Zozo."

"Why?"

"You see, Jojo," Popo explained, lowering his voice, "every so often we must decide who will lead us. We do so by voting. Our vote is what determines who we send to Parliament."

"Where *is* Parliament?" Jojo asked again.

"Well . . ." Popo the Wise scratched his head thoughtfully. "The last time I saw it, Parliament was that way. Or was it that way? I haven't been to the city for a long time. Let's go and see if it's still where I left it."

He made a short hop, flapped his wings, and took to the air. A black feather floated to the ground.

"You've lost a feather," Jojo called out.

There was no answer, so Jojo flapped his wings and

took off after him. Popo the Wise circled uncertainly for a moment, then flew straight southwards.

"Is it far?" Jojo asked.

"We shall see," Popo said. "Follow me."

Another black feather drifted past Jojo's head.

"That's not mine," Popo called, flying on.

It was followed by a white one and then a grey one.

"Not mine," said Popo again.

More feathers came flying towards them, of all sizes and colours, and they appeared so many and so fast that the old crow was worried.

"This is not a good sign," he said to Jojo. "This is not good at all."

Then they saw the source of the feathers. Up ahead was a huge flock of birds squawking and shoving and pecking. They were all over the sky, chasing one another and pulling out one another's feathers.

"Some birds can't disagree without pulling feathers," Popo explained to Jojo. "But they will be friends again once the election is over."

The noise the birds were making was enough to frighten Jojo.

"Don't worry," Popo said to him. "This way."

He turned and swooped down to the ground. Jojo landed next to him on the road to the city, and they started their long walk to their destination. Soon they came across a crowd of ravens shouting, "Raven rules! Raven rules!"

The ravens were stopping passersby and making them hop on one foot, singing, "Raven! Raven! Raven!"

"It is the election fever," Popo told Jojo as he joined the dancers. "Do as I do and follow me."

Jojo began to hop on one foot, shouting, "Raven! Raven! Raven!" and he followed Popo the Wise, dancing and singing his way through the crowd.

After they had passed the ravens, Popo and Jojo ran into a group of eagles armed with sticks and shrieking, "Eagle! Eagle! Eagle!" Like the ravens, the eagles stopped anyone who came by and made them dance and sing "Eagle! Eagle! Eagle!" Anyone who refused was roughed up and pushed about. There was no way of avoiding them, and once again Popo and Jojo had to dance their way through.

After the eagles came the hawks, and after them the vultures, singing and dancing and forcing everyone else to sing and dance with them. The air was full of music and song. Feathers flew in the wind: blue feathers, green feathers, black, white, and grey.

This is fun, Jojo thought, but Popo the Wise was becoming exhausted.

Eventually they reached their destination. The city streets were crowded and noisy; shops were closed and barred. All the different groups of birds stalked up and down, waving placards and dancing.

Popo the Wise landed on a tower to rest, and Jojo perched next to him. "I haven't danced so much since the last election," admitted the older crow.

A gang of hawks passed below them, shouting, "Vote for Hawk!"

On the next road more eagles were busy forcing everyone to sing "Vote for Eagle! Vote for Eagle!"

And the ravens were patrolling the street after that, organizing a chant of "Vote for Raven!"

The different groups clashed and argued. They all wanted to be heard.

"This is one time when everyone has a voice," said Popo the Wise. "We all get a chance to say who we want as our leader."

"All of us?"

"All grown-ups," Popo said. "We mark the name of our favourite candidate on a voting slip."

"Uncle Zozo?" asked Jojo.

"Yes, or anyone else."

"Uncle Dodo?"

"He's not a leader," said Popo the Wise. "Dodo just talks big. You choose someone who can lead, someone who does what he says, not one who just tells others what to do. You want someone good and wise. Someone good for all."

"Even an eagle?"

"Anyone," said Popo.

Jojo had heard so much about it that day that he had begun to think it was a family matter.

"Uncle Zozo would not like it if we didn't vote for him."

"Uncle Zozo would not know," said Popo. "No one would know, unless you told them."

Now he knew that it was not for crows alone, but Jojo still did not know where Parliament was.

Then Popo the Wise shielded his eyes and gazed about. "There!" he shouted. "Exactly where I left it. That big house is the House of Parliament."

Jojo looked where Popo's wing was pointing to a huge house on the hill.

"That is where Uncle Zozo wants to go," Popo said. "But he cannot unless we vote for him."

"Will you?"

Popo paused and then said, "I do not think he is the right bird for the job."

On the street below, a procession of chickens went by, clucking, "Vote for Chicken! Vote for Chicken!"

"The *chickens*?" Jojo asked in disbelief.

"Everyone has a right to be chosen," said Popo. "Just

as everyone has a right to choose. The one with the most votes will be the leader, and he will sit inside that big house with others and form a government. As you can see, it is not an easy process. The eagles want an eagle and the ducks want a duck. Hawks want a hawk and crows want a crow. And everyone has a right to take part. One day I'll tell you the story of how a chicken beat a hawk. But now it's getting late, and we have far to go. Follow me."

And with that, he flapped his wings and headed home. Jojo lingered for a moment, imagining himself in Parliament, then took off after Popo the Wise.

ARTICLE 21

WE ALL HAVE THE RIGHT TO TAKE PART IN THE GOVERNMENT OF OUR COUNTRY. GOVERNMENTS SHOULD BE VOTED FOR REGULARLY AND ALL ADULTS SHOULD HAVE THE RIGHT TO A VOTE. VOTING SHOULD BE SECRET AND ALL VOTES SHOULD BE EQUAL.

WHEREVER I LAY DOWN MY HEAD

Jamila Gavin

PADMA was the youngest aunt. Perhaps that was why, of all her mother's numerous sisters, Leela loved her the best: she was only a year or two older than Leela, and whenever the family went to India from London to visit the relatives, it was Padma she couldn't wait to see.

Padma was still a teenager—still funny, cheeky, and daring. She loved racing off with her English niece: introducing her to her friends, sipping sodas and eating pastries in the coffeehouses, window-shopping in the town centre. "Don't you dare call me Aunty," she scolded as Leela teased her and called her Aunty P. "Everyone will think I'm old!"

Sometimes when they had ordered too many pastries, they would give the remains to the street dwellers who often hung around the restaurants. One evening, Leela noticed an entire family—a poverty-stricken mother, father, young girl, and babe in arms—shuffling aimlessly along the pavement, and she wondered where they would sleep that night. They paused before a shop window full of rows of televisions dancing with images of beautiful houses and well-fed people advertising fast cars, kitchen gadgets, the finest butter for your child, the best food for your health, and lotions for your skin, your hair, your body. The family stood for a long time, silently staring, before finally drifting on.

"I wonder where they live," Leela murmured.

"Wherever they lay down their heads," replied Padma blithely. "Now, come on, let's get home! You can't solve all the world's problems."

Catching a motor-scooter rickshaw home, the girls shrieked with terrified laughter as the driver raced with death-defying bravado through the bazaar traffic, Leela screaming, "Oh, save me, Aunty!"

Leela was amazed how easily Padma, whenever they were invited to weddings and parties, could transform from a trendy teenager in jeans and logo-designed T-shirts into an elegant young woman in glistening saris or *sal-war kameez*, tinkling with jewels and glowing with carefully applied makeup. Then she really did look like an aunt, and Leela loved it when Padma hauled her to her bedroom to make her try on one outfit after another, until she pronounced on the one that suited Leela best, the one she should wear to the next wedding.

There was nothing like an Indian wedding party, though Aunty P loved to mock the couples mercilessly, whispering, "Why on earth did she agree to marry him? Look at him— going to seed already. I'd never marry just for a man's bank account." Or, "Poor Lakshmi, such a spoilt little thing! He's going to have his hands full with her, I can tell you."

They always exchanged shoals of e-mails when Leela returned to England, full of gossip and chatter. Aunty P told her about her growing social life: how she was meeting more and more people, especially boys! Soon she was writing about one in particular.

Rusty! That's what they call him. He's a hill boy from Assam. I love him, Leela, but don't you dare tell anyone. They would be so disapproving. Talk about racism! Why do our family think people from the hills are from another planet? Mummy and Daddy have picked out a boy for me already—but he's soooooo boring. I'll tell them about Rusty, but not just yet. I won't be marrying till after university, anyway—I can tell them then.

Padma's "Mummy and Daddy" were Leela's grandparents, and when they both died suddenly, one after the other, it was a terrible shock. Leela's mother wept with anguish. E-mails and phone calls flew across the ocean, and Leela's parents hurriedly booked air tickets to fly over first for one funeral and then, within three months, the second.

"It was such a love match," Leela's mother told her sadly when they returned. "When your grandmother fell ill and died, Grandfather couldn't live without her. They all say he died of a broken heart."

"Poor Aunty P! She's an orphan now," whispered Leela, and then realized that so, too, was her mother. "Poor Mum," she cried, hugging her close. "But will Aunty P be all right?"

In due course, Leela had an e-mail from Padma to say she had been taken in by her grandparents on her father's side, Leela's great-grandparents. Padma had begged to be allowed to live with one of her sisters, but the eldest, Leela's mother, was in Britain, and the rest were married and scattered across India, all of them much too far away from her school. It was agreed that Padma must put her education first. After all, as everyone said, without a good education she would never get a good husband.

At least it won't be too long before Aunty P goes away to university, thought Leela, remembering how strict and old-fashioned her great-grandparents were.

As Leela feared, Padma had a hard time settling down into the old-fashioned rural farming household after the noise and excitement of the city and all the independence she had been used to. Her grandfather's farm was marooned in an ocean of wheat fields, several miles outside the city, which meant she had to be driven to school and back each day—and no matter how hard she pleaded to be allowed to meet up with her friends after school, even when one of their brothers said he could drive her back on his moped, Grandfather always said no. And no meant no. And no meant she hardly ever saw Rusty.

As the farm had no e-mail connection, Padma had to use an Internet café near her school to send moaning e-mails to Leela.

They're so traditional. They won't let me go any-where unaccompanied. I never go to movies now, or see my friends in the coffee shops. I hate being in the middle of nowhere. I feel as though I'm suffocating. Thank goodness for e-mail—at least I can stay in touch with you, and with Rusty. I still love him, you know, and he loves me. We've promised each other we'll get married as soon as I'm through university.

But some of her e-mails were desperate, full of sorrow for her parents, full of longing to be free from the stifling life she now led, and Leela wished she were nearer to comfort her. So she was thrilled when her parents sent her out to the farm for a short holiday. She couldn't wait to see Padma again, even though it would be at her great-grandparents' home in the middle of nowhere.

She was so relieved to find Aunty P just the same: still the laughing girl with flashing bold eyes, daring her niece into mischief. Throughout her stay Padma never grumbled or huffed or sighed as she had in her e-mails. "I go to university in a month, and then I'll be *freeeee!*" she whispered jubilantly.

The girls had fun during those two short weeks, chatting nonstop and giggling over the silliest things. Perhaps because of Leela, Grandfather shrugged and relaxed his vigilance a little, allowing the two of them to take the car sometimes and go off sightseeing with a driver.

So Leela returned to England reassured. She never saw the sparkle die from Aunty P's eyes, or her head, usually tossed back with laughter, bow submissively when, after Leela had gone, Grandfather told Padma that rather than go to university as planned, which would cost such a lot of money, she should marry Hari, the man her parents had chosen for her long ago. Hari had agreed to marry her immediately. And after all, he was so well off, what need was there for a university degree when she would never have to go out to work as so many modern girls did these days?

Leela and her parents flew out for the wedding. Wandering among the glittering guests, Leela listened wryly to other young girls whispering the same sort of caustic remarks that she and Padma used to mutter at weddings.

"Not exactly Bollywood, is he! A bit of a drip; look at his sticky-out ears; he won't be much of a laugh. Oh, well, he's supposed to be very rich. I expect she'll live like a queen."

"I hope so," sighed Leela, who couldn't help silently agreeing with them, and hoped that her gift to Padma of a pair of turquoise earrings wouldn't be deemed too modest.

Leela barely had a chance to talk to Aunty P. She lined up before the wedding thrones with five hundred or so other guests to congratulate the bride and groom, and Padma, as she tipped her powdered cheek for Leela to kiss, whispered, "Don't ever lose me," and Leela thought that such a strange thing to say.

Yet, before even a year was out, Aunty P was lost.

What a scandal her disappearance caused! She had left her husband's beautiful house, and the lavish lifestyle he provided, and just gone. At first, gossip spread like wildfire: she had run off with a hill boy, abandoned her husband for some poverty-stricken somebody or other she had met in a coffee shop. But then there came a more terrible explanation. Her husband had discovered an e-mail from Rusty. Hari had accused Padma of being unfaithful, and when it transpired that she was pregnant, he had declared that the child couldn't possibly be his and had kicked her out of his house.

"Kicked her out?" Leela was aghast. "Aunty P would have told me if she had been seeing Rusty. She told me everything. I don't believe it."

Leela was grilled by her parents. "You two were like this," cried her mother, holding up two crossed fingers. "Did she mention this hill boy? Is there any truth in it? Didn't she say anything in one of her e-mails?"

Reluctantly Leela told her that yes, before Aunty P was married, she had been in love with another boy—yes, he was from the hills, and they had talked of marriage—but once Padma had obediently married the man her parents had chosen, the hill boy had gone back home. Leela was sure Padma would never have stayed in touch with Rusty, let alone become pregnant by him.

"Surely if Aunty P had it in her to run away," she argued, "she would have done so before she got married, not after?"

Leela sent e-mail after e-mail, hoping that Padma would reply. But there was silence. It was as if she had vanished from the face of the earth.

Leela's mother wept with fury and anxiety for her little sister. "How could she be so stupid? How could she dishonour us like this?"

Leela was overwhelmed with guilt. If only she'd realized how unhappy her aunt had been. If only she'd been more sensitive. Padma must have been desperate. Where was she?

Leela begged her parents to go back to India to try to find her. "She's your own sister, Mum! Don't you care?"

Of course she cared, but she believed what everyone else in the family believed—that Padma had run away with Rusty. "Your aunty P always was a rebel, always reading those magazines and things. As Grandfather says, she's made her bed and must lie in it—and everyone listens to Grandfather."

"Besides, it would be like looking for a needle in a haystack," argued Leela's father. "In any case, we can't just up sticks and go. She'll show up, just you see."

"Stop worrying," said her mother. "Your aunty P's a survivor, believe me."

Then news came that Aunty P had turned up at a sister's house in the south and had begged to be allowed to stay. She'd claimed her husband had become violent and jealous and had refused to believe that the baby was his. He had disowned her and her unborn child.

Despite Padma's insisting on her innocence and pleading

for help, brother-in-law told her she had to leave. Whatever the truth of it, she had brought shame on the entire family. No one would take her in.

"Go home, Padma! Make peace with your husband. He's the one you must persuade. You have no other choice."

Padma must have felt such terror, Leela thought—so much so that she couldn't face going back. Leela could hardly bear to imagine it.

"See if the grandparents will have you, then," her brother-in-law had said, but a telephone call had ascertained, categorically, that they wanted nothing more to do with her. They had always known she was a little minx, and even blamed her English niece for being a bad influence.

"She doesn't deserve a home. Let her live on the streets. It's where she belongs!"

"You'd better go and find this Rusty," her brother-in-law had said then. "You can't stay here. We don't have the room, especially if you're having a baby."

But Padma's sister had fallen at his feet and beseeched him to let her stay—just for a while. There had been a quarrel, tears, and raised voices, until brother-in-law had relented and agreed that Padma could stay for a week to sort herself out. She could sleep on the sofa in the living room.

By morning she had gone.

*　　*　　*

Three years went by, but there was hardly a day when Leela didn't wonder what had happened to her aunt. Was she all right? What about her baby? How was she living? Why did no one know or care? Her mother was tight-lipped and wouldn't discuss it, while Leela raged helplessly. She hated and despised the family out there for not giving Padma a home; she hated that their idea of honour was greater than their compassion for one of their own. Leela's father at least wrote and offered to bring Padma to England, but by that time, no one knew where she was.

Leela sent off e-mail after e-mail, begging Padma to reply, but once they started bouncing back, she knew it was useless and stopped trying. All she could feel was a deep sadness—and sometimes resentment—that their friendship hadn't been strong enough, after all, for Aunty P to have confided in her or at least to have told her she was all right.

But that year—her gap year before going to university—Leela finally managed to return to India, taking up a job at an ashram for the elderly. She worked a whole year but only made one courtesy visit to see her great-grandparents. She hated their critical eyes and their unspoken disapproval, and she felt accused, that it was she who was somehow responsible for Padma's fall from grace. She was tired of hearing them blame the evil influence of the West and had to bite her lip not to argue with them.

Instead, during breaks in her work, Leela travelled, getting to know the country by bus and train, her eyes constantly scanning the world around her in case she saw her aunt. How often she cried out her name—"Aunty P!"—if she glimpsed a woman on the street, caught in a flash of sunlight a twist of the head or a movement of an arm that, for a second, looked like Padma but then wasn't. Leela even took a bus up into the Assam hills, fantasizing that perhaps Aunty P had indeed found her beloved Rusty and was living happily ever after.

Leela had come to a small rural station for an overnight train to take her back to the ashram. It was evening: not like the softness of an English dusk fading to night, but a violent Indian evening—a cacophony of noise and colour from nature, man, and beast. The sun was a blazing orb behind a dark line of trees, first fiery gold, turning to shimmering silver. Stray dogs huddled down into the earth for the night. Rooks and starlings whirled like dervishes in the dying sky; they screamed and quarrelled and squabbled among the branches as they fought for space to roost.

The train came in, and there was a flurry of activity as the gaunt rickshaw drivers vied for a fare among the cluster of passengers who got off. Leela found her compartment and sat by the grimy window watching it all, watching the remaining rickshaw drivers settle themselves into their own cycle rickshaws, which would be their bed until the next train came in, their feet up on the handlebars, their heads flung back. Home for man and beast was wherever you could lay down your head.

Leela's attention turned to a slow-moving woman and child who came drifting into the forecourt. A shabby sari was wound around the woman's body and head. She shielded her face behind the thin cotton with one hand, while in the other she carried a bundle on her shoulder. The child, a small scraggy girl, wore a dusty pair of pyjamas and tunic, her hair hanging down her back in neat but dull plaits. She wandered listlessly ahead of her mother, suddenly pointing out a space beyond the line of rickshaws.

With barely a nod of acknowledgement, the woman went to the place the child had indicated. She put down her bundle and carefully unfolded it. Out came a cooking pot, a tin, a smaller bundle into which were folded a few chapattis, a bottle of water, a metal beaker, and a plate. As the child squatted down, the woman gave her a chapatti to chew while she proceeded to shake out the cloth that had formed the larger bundle. It was the size of a shawl, but she spread it across the dusty ground for another purpose and meticulously smoothed it out, lining up one corner with the next as though it was of the greatest importance to have each corner properly aligned. It seemed to Leela that the woman took an inordinate amount of time and trouble arranging the shawl and fixing its corners with piles of stones that she collected at random. By the time she had finished, the child had eaten her portion of chapatti and drunk from the water bottle.

The woman beckoned the child, lifted her onto the shawl, and laid her down.

The whistle blew, and the train eased away just as the woman pulled the sari off her head. She unwound enough to wrap the child into the warmth of her body as she, too, stretched herself out to sleep. Something made the woman sit up and shake out her hair, and Leela glimpsed her earrings with a shock of recognition. They were the ones she had given Padma on her wedding day. Briefly the woman turned, and her gaunt, weathered face, aged before her time, was clearly visible.

"Padma! Aunty P!"

Leela hammered on the sealed glass as the train gathered speed. She hurled herself at the door and pulled down the window, still screaming into the rushing air, "Don't go away! I'm coming back for you!" as the two diminishing figures, who were now just specks, laid down their heads.

ARTICLE 22
WE ALL HAVE THE RIGHT TO A HOME.

CHRISTOPHER

Eoin Colfer

MARCO dreamt of lying in fat green grass and gazing up at blue sky. Sometimes the dream was so solid in his mind that he thought it must have actually happened. In another life, maybe.

A spool of thread came flying through the air and hit him on the forehead.

"You dreaming about grass again?"

Christopher. Of course. The Kenyan boy's smile was white in his dark face.

"Grass? Grass like fat worms?"

"Caterpillars, *stupido,*" corrected Marco.

Christopher frowned. "*Cat hair peelers? You* are *stupido,* Marco baby."

Marco chuckled twice. It took a lot to drag two chuckles out of a person in this place, but Christopher could do it.

"*You* are the *stupido,* Christopher *baby.* And you stink like the backside of a sick dog."

Now Christopher chuckled. "Backside of a sick dog. This is a prince among insults."

Heavy footsteps creaked on the floorboards, and the boys stopped their joking. Bluto was on the work floor. The factory foreman honked into his phone for a minute, then hung up, muttering angrily. This was a dangerous time. Bluto fined people when he was upset.

Marco hunched low into his work, shutting out the universe. This was what Bluto wanted to see in his employees: "a good work ethic."

On this Sunday, Marco was stitching gold wings onto the pockets of fake Nike shorts. The wing was the adopted symbol of the AC Milan striker Costas Andioni.

"Andioni breaks his leg, and we're gonna be picking these wings out with our teeth," Christopher whispered just loudly enough for everyone to hear, earning himself a clout on the ear and yet another visit to the office.

Mrs. M left the door open so the workers could hear what happened to smart-mouths.

"This ain't no sweatshop, Kenya," she shouted, her shrill voice rising to the concrete ceiling. "You're free to go anytime you want. You want to go, go. You going, Kenya?"

Christopher shook his head, chin so low it touched his chest.

Marco caught his breath. *They have broken him,* he thought. *Even brave, shining Christopher.*

But when Christopher returned to his bench, the first thing he did was ask whether Marco had farted.

Marco smiled. *Still Christopher!*

Bluto growled at him. "What you smiling at, kid? You don't get no extra time for smiling. Stitch them wings speedy, the way I like it."

Marco never offered backchat; he could not afford to be docked an hour's pay. Bluto loved to dock wages. Christopher said that whatever Bluto took from you, he kept for himself to buy rare Pokémon cards for his collection. Everyone pulled their weight in Marco's family; even the twins helped to make the foil roses that his mother sold at the city's traffic lights.

"Speedy, Mr. Bluto," Marco replied, disliking the man even as he smiled. "Just the way you like it."

And so he worked that day. Wing after wing. Gold thread on the inside, red flames feathered around the border. Marco worked without a break until dusk, until his backbone was a glowing rod and his fingers were claws.

Eventually he leant back and sighed, his breath pluming like chimney smoke. Mrs. M always turned off the heat around midday, claiming that the workers' own industry should keep them warm.

The toilet door was open a crack, and he could see that the cramped room was unoccupied for once; this was an opportunity not to be missed. Marco pushed back his chair, tugged at his cushion to make sure it was tied down securely, then walked stiffly towards the bathroom.

In spite of the factory's chill, a dense smell clogged the building. There was bleach in the mix, and sweat, rubber, and oil. Though he knew it was merely a blend of chemicals, Marco imagined the smell was alive. He could use this in one of his stories.

Marco often wrote stories, most featuring Quantum Boy (Marco himself) and his sidekick, Dreadlock (Christopher, of course). Quantum Boy zipped through time, getting himself entangled in historical adventures, and Dreadlock was always on hand with a witty comment at the right moment. Such as, "This time you have come up short, Napoleon."

Marco hurried towards the vacant bathroom. There were dozens of workers in the factory at any time and only one toilet, so it was wise to take advantage whenever it was free. Bluto had pinned up a bathroom timetable, but even he could not control nature's call. Marco ducked quickly inside. He did not pull the bulb cord, because then Mr. Bluto would see the light leaking out under the door and come to hurry him along.

The bathroom was colder than the rest of the factory because it wasn't really part of the building. There was a gap one block wide between the bathroom and the outer factory wall, where the cinder blocks had subsided from the factory proper. The wind whistled through and froze the toilet seat.

Marco twisted his neck, clicking it, a habit his mother hated.

"You want to end up stuck like that? Always looking up? Find a job then, little Marco, for a looking-up person."

"Air-traffic controller," his sister had said, quick as a flash. Little Mira was one smart girl.

And as Marco smiled at this memory, he did not notice the *click-clack* of Bluto's approaching footsteps. And because there was no light seeping out under the door, Bluto presumed the bathroom was empty.

He barrelled into the cramped space backwards, shouting into his phone. "I said Tropical Mega Battle, gold edition, you idiot. Not bronze. I won't pay a penny for bronze!"

Bluto did not realize Marco was there until he sat on him. Even then he did not know it was Marco, because if he had, he surely would not have run out onto the work floor with his trousers in his hand, screaming, "Toilet monster! It bit me. They *are* real. I knew it. I knew it!"

The experience was not pleasant for Marco, either. One second his life did not seem to be in any immediate danger, and the next, there was a sudden overpowering smell of sweat and cheese and his face was being mashed by back fat.

Marco stumbled out into the factory, squinting and gasping like a prisoner released from his dungeon.

"Sorry," he coughed, knowing that whatever had happened would be his fault. "I'm sorry, sir. I must hurry back to work."

Bluto lurched forward, grabbing Marco's shoulder. "Tell them, boy. You must have felt it. You must have . . ." He stuttered to a halt as the truth became clear. It had been Marco in the bathroom with the lights off. Only Marco. "No toilet monster," the foreman breathed, calming himself with gulps of air. "Just a boy."

And for a moment, he was relieved; then the red tint of embarrassment coloured his cheeks.

By now every worker in the factory had gathered around—even Mrs. M had come out of her office to check on the disturbance. She stood, wrapped in her knee-length puffa jacket, glaring at the foreman.

"When I was a child," explained Bluto, "my brother told me stories of a monster who lived in the toilet bowl . . ." It sounded ridiculous, even to his own ears. "This boy!" he shouted, hoisting his trousers with one hand. "Skulking in the bathroom with the light off. He must be docked! Fired!"

Marco paled.

Christopher piped up from the throng of workers. "The toilet monster. He is the one who must be fired."

A few workers tittered, but not Bluto. "Shut your mouth, Kenya. This boy must go."

"But if Marco goes, who will stitch Andioni's wings?" asked Christopher. "The toilet monster? His fingers are clumsy and he will drip on the material."

More laughter now—even Mrs. M's mouth was twitching at one corner.

"Please, Mrs. M," pleaded Bluto. "Fire him now."

Christopher contorted his face and limbs in a hilarious impression of a dull monster trying to sew. "*Arrrrrgh!* Dis work be berry difficult for poor toilet monster."

Bluto charged at Christopher. The other workers clapped and whooped as the young African boy easily dodged the foreman, weaving between the machines. The fun might have lasted longer had Mrs. M not anticipated Christopher's route and snagged him by the ear as he shot round a corner.

"That's the end of your little game, Kenya," she snapped. "Into the office with you."

Bluto was still in attack mode, but Mrs. M froze him with a single pointed finger. "And you! Prepare my peppermint tea. And in the future, whistle before entering the bathroom. Everyone knows the toilet monster cannot bear whistling."

"A good joke, Mrs. M," said Christopher, smiling.

Mrs. M shrank his smile with another tug on the ear, dragging the skinny boy towards her office, where he would surely be fired.

Marco did not know what to do. Quantum Boy would blast Mrs. M into the dinosaur age, but Marco had no special powers. He was a scared boy who still hadn't been to the toilet. Though he felt a little guilty, Marco backed into the bathroom, remembering to switch on the light. Out of the corner of his eye, he saw something move. Mrs. M. Her office window could be clearly seen through the gap between bathroom and factory wall.

Before Marco knew what he was doing, his arm was through the gap, seeming to pull the rest of him after it. It was a tight squeeze, but he sucked in his rib cage, flattened his nose, and managed to inch through the gap until he emerged into the factory yard. The sky was wrong. Where there should have been the dark blue of night, there were orange-bellied clouds reflecting the city's streetlights.

Go back, whispered Marco's good sense. *Go back.*

But he did not.

The window blinds were old and missing several slats, so Marco's view was barely obstructed. He made a funnel with his hands and looked through it to the room inside.

Mrs. M was behind her desk, yelling at Christopher, who sat in a wooden chair facing her. She shouted and pounded the desk, making the pens jump.

I must call out to him, thought Marco. *Share the blame. Perhaps Mrs. M could fine us both and fire neither.*

But then Marco noticed that something was not right. Mrs. M smiled and even winked at Christopher, who did not seem in the least afraid. As a matter of fact, he seemed comfortable and relaxed, propping his knees on the desk and helping himself to some peanuts from a bowl.

Marco moved further along, to a spot where the pane was cracked and a dagger-shaped sliver of glass had fallen out.

"Another incident like this and you will be let go, Kenya!" he heard Mrs. M say.

"Thank you, madam," Christopher replied, his white, even teeth like rows of chewing gum. "I will be a good worker."

It was all fake, Marco realized with surprise. For the benefit of those listening on the factory floor.

Mrs. M spoke again, this time in quiet tones. "You go too far with Bluto," she said. "Your job is to keep the workers happy. Happy workers are hard workers."

"Bluto was scaring Marco," said Christopher. "He is

the best worker we have. A big joke was needed to calm everyone."

Mrs. M seemed impressed by such wisdom. "You are right, dear Christopher. If Marco had gone, ten more would have followed him and then the Andioni order would never be finished on time." She opened her desk drawer and counted out a few notes. "A small bonus for my Trojan horse."

Christopher took the money and tucked it into his sock. "You should tell Bluto to leave Marco alone. He is soft, but he is my friend."

"I will tell him. Now, you go back to work."

"Five more minutes, a can of Pepsi?"

Mrs. M smiled almost tenderly. "One can. Five minutes, then you leave here crying like a baby."

He pushed out his bottom lip. "No one cries like Christopher," he said. Then, in a typical Christopher motion, he popped out of the chair like a circus acrobat and across to a small fridge. He selected a cola and stretched out on the floor to drink it.

"Drink slowly," Mrs. M chided. "Or you will give yourself a tummy ache."

Christopher's reply was a gentle burp.

Marco turned away from the window. His friend's job was safe; that much was clear. But was his friend his friend?

Dreadlock is gone, he realized. *There is only Quantum*

Boy now. And Marco felt cold and betrayed. Christopher had been masquerading as their comedian, when all the time he was under Mrs. M's wing.

Even so, I still laughed. Does it matter why he jokes?

It did matter, he decided. Christopher's jokes were like glossy red apples with black sludge at their core. He would not laugh again.

Marco felt sick to his stomach and wished that he could go home. But he knew he must return to the factory. Before he went back inside, he allowed himself one last longing look at the lights and life of the city beyond. His mother was out there somewhere, selling foil roses at the traffic lights of East London.

ARTICLE 24
WE ALL HAVE THE RIGHT TO REST FROM WORK AND RELAX.

NO TRUMPETS NEEDED

Michael Morpurgo

I am a cameraman. I work freelance, on my own; it's how I like it. I was on the West Bank a few weeks ago, my first job in the cauldron of contention that is the Middle East. Of course, I had seen on television, like most of us, the anguish of the grieving, the burnt-out buses, the ritual humiliation of checkpoints, the tanks in the streets, the stone-throwing crowds, the olive groves and the hilltop settlements, children playing in open sewers in the refugee camps—and now the wall. The wall to separate Palestinian from Israeli, Arab from Jew. I knew the place in images; I was there to make more of them, I suppose. And I wanted to find out the effect the wall was having on the people who lived close to it—on both sides. I began my travels on the Palestinian side.

I had been there only a couple of days when I first came across the shepherd boy. He was sitting alone on a hillside under an olive tree, his sheep grazing all around him. I had seen nothing remotely picturesque in this land until that moment, nothing until now that reminded me in any way of its biblical past. The shepherd boy was making a kite, so intent upon it that he had not noticed my approach. He was whistling softly—not to make a tune, I felt, but simply to reassure his sheep. When he did look up, he showed no surprise or alarm. His smile was openhearted and engaging, so much so that I could not bring myself to pass by with a mere greeting or paltry nod of the head.

I sat down and offered him a drink out of my ruck-sack. He drank gratefully, eagerly, but said nothing. I patted my camera, told him who I was, shook his hand. I tried to communicate in English, then in the very few words of Arabic I had picked up. His smile was the only reply I got. He seemed to like me there, wanted me to stay, but I could tell he didn't understand a word I was saying. So after a while I lapsed into silence and watched him at work on his kite, the sheep shifting all around us under the shade of the tree, their smell pungent and heavy in the warm air.

When I began to film him he seemed unconcerned, dis-interested even. We shared what food we had. He took a great fancy to some Scottish shortbread I'd brought with me from back home, and he gave me some of his pine nuts.

We shared our silence, too, both of us knowing instinctively that this was fine, as good a way as any to get to know each other.

When evening came and he stood up and began to whistle his sheep home, it seemed natural for me to go with him, like one of his flock. Later, I found myself sitting in his house, surrounded by his huge extended family, all talking among themselves and watching me, if not with hostility, certainly with some suspicion. It was an unsettling experience. But the boy, I noticed, still said nothing. He was showing everyone the progress he had made with his kite; I could see that he was a treasured child.

We ate lamb and the most succulent broad beans I had ever tasted, then sweet spiced cake dripping with honey. When the boy came and sat down beside me, it was as if he was showing me off. I was his guest, and I felt suddenly honoured by that and moved by his affection.

Then, much to my surprise, one of the men spoke to me directly and in good English. "I am Said's uncle," he began. "You are most welcome in our home. Said would want to say this himself, but he does not speak. Not any longer. I remember there was a time when you could not stop him."

He would pause occasionally to explain to everyone what he was telling me.

"It happened two years ago," he went on. "Mahmoud

was flying his kite on the hill. It was before they built the wall. Mahmoud was Said's elder brother. He loved to make kites. He loved to fly kites. Said was with him; he was always with him. That day, a settler's car had been ambushed down in the valley. Three of them were killed; one was a little girl. Afterwards the soldiers came, and the helicopters. There was some shooting. Perhaps it was a revenge killing, or maybe it was a stray bullet. Who knows? Who cares? Mahmoud was shot dead, and Said saw it all. In front of his eyes he saw it.

"Since this day he does not speak; since this day he does not grow. God willing, he will. God willing. It is true that he is small, that he cannot speak, but he is the best shepherd in all Palestine. He makes the best kites, too. And I tell you something: Said's kites are no ordinary kites."

"What do you mean?" I asked.

"Maybe he will show you that himself tomorrow. Maybe he will fly his kite for you. This one is almost ready, I think. But the wind must always be from the east, or Said will not fly his kites."

I spent the night on the roof of the house, under the stars, tired but far too troubled to sleep. I woke at dawn and went down into the valley to film the sun rising over the wall. Once I'd done that, I climbed back up the hill to get a long tracking shot of the wall as it sliced through the olive groves and across the hillside beyond. Dogs barked, and cocks crowed at one another from both sides of the wall.

After breakfast I set off with Said and his sheep, Said carrying his kite, now with string attached. I doubted he'd be flying it that day, as there was very little wind. But an hour or so later, sitting on the highest hill above the village, with the sheep browsing in among the rocks, their bells sounding softly, I felt a sudden breeze spring up. Said was on his feet at once, eagerly offering me his kite. I noticed then that there was writing on one side, and a drawing too, of a dove.

He was urging me to run now, racing ahead to show me how to do it. I felt the wind taking it, felt the kite suddenly wind-whipped and tugging to be free. Said clapped his hands in wild delight as it swooped and soared above us. I had done this on Hampstead Heath with my father when I was a boy, but had forgotten the sheer exhilaration of it. The kite was alive at the end of the string, loving it as much as I was. Said tugged my arm and took the string from me. Reluctantly I handed it over.

Said was an expert. With a tweak of his wrist, the kite turned and twirled; with a flick of his fingers, it dived and danced. My professional instinct kicked in. I needed boy and kite in the same shot, so I had to put some distance between them and me. I backed away over the hillside, pausing to film as I went, fearful of missing these fleeting moments of innocent rapture in this war-ravaged land. I closed on the fluttering kite, then zoomed in on the wall below, following it up over the hill and focusing on the settlement beyond, on the blue-and-white flag flying there, and then on some children playing football in the street below. I watched them through my lens, witnessed the celebrations as one of them scored. I turned my camera on Said again. There was, I noticed, a look of intense concentration on his face.

That was the moment he let the kite go. It was quite deliberate. He simply gave it to the wind, holding his arms aloft as if he were releasing a trapped bird, giving it its freedom. It soared up high, seeming to float there for a while on the thermal before the wind discovered it and took it away over the olive grove, over the wall, and up towards the hilltop settlement.

Said was tugging at my arm again. He wanted to see through my lens. I saw then what he was looking at: a young girl in a headscarf gazing up at the kite as it came floating down. Running to where it landed, she picked it up and stood watching us for a moment, before the footballers came racing down the hill towards her. They all stood there then and gazed across at us. But when Said waved, only the girl waved back. They didn't fly the kite. They just took it away and disappeared.

On the way home with the sheep later that day, we

came across Said's uncle harvesting his broad beans. "It's a poor crop, but what can you do?" he said to me. "There's never enough water. The Israelis, settlers, call them what you will, they take all our best land, all our water, and leave us only the dust to farm in."

I stopped to talk while Said walked on up into the village with his sheep.

"So the wind was right," Said's uncle continued. "Said never keeps his kites, you know, not one. He just makes them, waits for the east wind, and sends them off. Did you see what he draws on each one? A dove of peace. Did you see what he writes? It is in Arabic and Hebrew. *Salaam. Shalom.*"

"How many has he sent?" I asked.

"A hundred, maybe. About one a week since they killed Mahmoud. He once wrote down for his mother why he does it. For Said, every kite that lands over there is like a seed of friendship. He believes that one day, they will send the kites back and everything will be right. Friendships will grow, and peace will come, and the killing will stop. Let him have his dream. It's all he has. He'll find out soon enough what they're like over there."

"There was a girl who found the kite," I told him. "She waved back. I saw her. It's a beginning."

"It costs nothing to wave," he replied bitterly.

I stayed one more night, so I was there to see the

embryo of the next kite taking shape: Said kneeling on the carpet, his whole family watching intently as he constructed the frame with infinite care, ignoring all their advice and all offers of food and drink.

"Maybe it is good," Said's uncle said to me later, when Said had gone up to bed. "Maybe it helps him to forget. Maybe if he forgets, he will find his voice again. Maybe he will grow again. God willing. God willing."

I said my good-byes to the family early the next morning and left with Said and the sheep. Said held my hand all the way. There was between us, I felt, the same unspoken thought: that we were friends and did not want to part, and that once we did we would probably never see each other again.

The sheep were in a clambering mood, their bells jangling loud in the morning air. We sat down on the hillside where we'd flown the kite the day before. Said had brought the frame of his new kite with him, but he was not in the mood for working on it. Like me, he was looking out over the valley, over the wall, towards the settlement. The blue-and-white flag still fluttered there. A donkey brayed balefully nearby, winding itself into a frenzy of misery. I felt it was time for me to go. I put my hand on Said's shoulder, let it rest there a moment, then left him.

When I looked back a while later, I saw he was busy with his kite, and I stopped to film him. It would be the perfect closing shot. I had just about got myself ready to film when Said sprang to his feet. His sheep were suddenly bounding away from him, scattering across the hillside.

Then I saw the kites. They were all colours of the rainbow, hundreds of them, like dancing butterflies rising into the air from the hillside below the settlement. I could hear the shrieks of joy, see the crowd of children gathered there, every one of them flying a kite. A few snagged on each other and plunged to earth, but most sailed triumphantly heavenwards. The settlers were pouring out of their houses to watch.

One after the other the kites were released, took wind, and flew out over the wall towards us. And from behind me, from Said's village, the people came running, too, as the kites landed among us, and among the terrified sheep. On every kite I recognized the same message, in Arabic and in Hebrew: *Salaam. Shalom.* And on every kite, too, there was a drawing of a dove holding an olive branch.

Everywhere on both sides of the wall, the children were cheering and laughing and dancing. I could see the girl in the scarf waving at us and leaping up and down.

Around me some of the mothers and fathers, grandmothers and grandfathers began to clap, too, hesitantly at first. Others soon joined in, Said's uncle among them. But the cheering, I noticed, and the laughter and the dancing, they left to the children. The hillside rang with their jubilation, with their exultation. It seemed to me like a symphony of hope.

As I raced back towards Said, I could hear him laughing and shouting aloud along with all the others. I realized then, idiot that I was, that I had quite forgotten to film this miracle. And almost immediately I understood that it didn't matter anyway, that it was the laughter that mattered. It was laughter that would one day resonate so loud that this wall would come tumbling down. No trumpets needed, as they had been at Jericho, only the laughter of children.

ARTICLE 28

WE HAVE A RIGHT TO PEACE AND ORDER SO THAT WE CAN ALL ENJOY RIGHTS AND FREEDOMS IN OUR OWN COUNTRY AND ALL OVER THE WORLD.

"NOBODY CAN TAKE THESE RIGHTS AND FREEDOMS FROM US."

ARTICLE 30
UNIVERSAL DECLARATION
OF HUMAN RIGHTS, 1948

Photo by Sara Jane Palmer

David Almond is the Carnegie, Whitbread, and Smarties Award-winning author of *Skellig*, *The Fire-Eaters*, *Clay*, *The Savage*, and many other novels, stories, picture books, and plays and is regarded as one of the most exciting and innovative children's authors writing today. His work has been translated into more than thirty languages and has been widely adapted for stage and screen. He lives with his family in Northumberland, England.

Ibtisam Barakat is a Palestinian author, poet, and educator living in the United States. She grew up under Israeli occupation and as a child found it utterly confusing to experience discrimination all the time. "As a teenager," she says, "when I found a copy of the UDHR at a UN office, I copied it by hand and kept it in my pocket. When Mother washed my pants and the paper tore up, I memorized it." Her memoir, *Tasting the Sky: A Palestinian Childhood*, has won numerous awards.

Malorie Blackman began her adult working life in computing, after which she considered acting before finally settling on writing books and scripts for children. She has since written more than fifty books, including *Pig-Heart Boy*, *Hacker*, and the hugely popular Noughts & Crosses series. In 2008, Malorie was awarded an OBE for services to children's literature. She lives in London with her husband and children.

Theresa Breslin lives in Scotland and is the critically acclaimed author of more than thirty books for children and young adults, many of which have won and been short-listed for awards, including the Carnegie Medal for her novel *Whispers in the Graveyard*. Her work has been filmed for television and broadcast on radio, and her books are read worldwide in more than twenty languages.

Eoin (pronounced "Owen") **Colfer** has written several best-selling children's novels, including the Artemis Fowl series, which has been translated into forty-two languages and has won several international awards. Eoin has always had a strong sense of fairness, and in response to Article 24, he wrote his story about the injustice of a child whose youth is cut short through no fault of his own. He also wanted to show that bad things can happen close to home as well as far away. He lives in Wexford, Ireland.

Roddy Doyle lives and works in Dublin. He is best known for his novels, plays, and screenplays for adults but has also written for children, including a humorous series of books about a dog called Rover. In 1993, his book *Paddy Clarke Ha Ha Ha* won the Booker Prize. In 1997, he won a tin of biscuits in a raffle.

Ursula Dubosarsky wanted to be a writer from an early age and is now the author of more than twenty books for children. She has won several national literary awards in her native Australia, and her work is published around the world. Ursula was interested in Article 12 because it is about privacy and the protection of your reputation. "These seem less dramatic, perhaps, than other human rights," she says, "but to me they're fundamental to your sense of who you are as a person."

Jamila Gavin was born in India but moved to the UK as a teenager. She has written numerous books for children of all ages, many of which have been inspired by her Indian roots. Her novel *Coram Boy*, which was published to great acclaim in 2000, won The Whitbread Children's Book Award, was short-listed for the Carnegie Medal, and was subsequently adapted for the stage.

Patricia McCormick worked as an investigative reporter and journalist before going on to write novels for young people. The third of these, *Sold*, was motivated by her passion for justice for women sold into sexual slavery in India and Nepal, and was a National Book Award Finalist. Patricia lives in New York with her husband, son, and two cats.

Margaret Mahy worked for many years as a librarian before eventually becoming a full-time children's author, and she has since been published all over the world. She has won many awards for both her picture books and fiction, most notably the Carnegie Medal twice, for *The Haunting* (1982) and *The Changeover* (1984), and her contribution to children's literature in her native New Zealand has been immense. Margaret lives near Christchurch, New Zealand, and when she is not writing, she enjoys trying to keep her pets and grandchildren in order.

Michael Morpurgo has an unparalleled reputation as a storyteller. He has written more than one hundred books for children, winning countless awards, including the Whitbread Children's Book Award, the Smarties Book Prize, the Blue Peter Book Award, and the Red House Children's Book Award. His books are translated and read around the world. Michael held the post of UK Children's Laureate in 2003–2005, and he and his wife, Clare, live in Devon, England.

After studying at the Royal College of Art, **Sarah Mussi** left the UK for Africa. She attended university in Nigeria, then lived in Cameroon and went on to raise her children in Ghana. She now lives in London and is the author of two novels for young adults, *The Door of No Return* and *The Last of the Warrior Kings*. Sarah sees her story, based on Article 7, as "a playful look at power and prejudice" and "a mischievous poke at British double standards."

Meja Mwangi is a prolific Kenyan novelist who has achieved worldwide recognition as an exciting and versatile writer. He was born in 1948 in Nanyuki, Kenya, and published his first novel, *Kill Me Quick,* in 1973. He has since gone on to write for both adults and children, with titles that include *The Mzungu Boy, The Boy Gift,* and *The Big Chiefs.* Much of Meja's writing has been inspired by his childhood in 1950s Kenya under a colonial government, and injustice is a common theme.

Rita Williams-Garcia lives in Jamaica, New York, and is the author of eight novels for young adults, all of which have been listed as ALA Best Books for Young Adults; *Like Sisters on the Homefront* was also named a Coretta Scott King Honor Book and received much critical attention. Rita currently teaches writing for children and young adults at Vermont College, Montpelier, and has two daughters.

Jacqueline Wilson is one of Britain's most outstanding writers for young readers. More than twenty-five million copies of her books have been sold in the UK alone, and they have been translated into thirty-four languages. Jacqueline has been honored with many of the UK's top awards, including the Guardian Children's Fiction Prize and the Smarties Book Prize. She was the UK Children's Laureate in 2005–2007 and became "Dame" Jacqueline Wilson in 2008. She lives in London.

THE UNIVERSAL DECLARATION OF HUMAN RIGHTS, 1948

We all have human rights, no matter who we are or where we live.

After the Holocaust and the horrors of the Second World War, world leaders came together to try to work out how to build peace. The Universal Declaration of Human Rights (UDHR) was written. It was the first international document to state that all human beings have fundamental rights and freedoms, and it is still one of the most famous and important of all human rights documents in the world.

Human rights are what every human being needs to live a life that is fair and respected, free from abuse, fear, and want, and to be free to express our own beliefs. Human rights belong to all of us, regardless of who we are or where we live—they are part of what makes us human. But they are not always respected.

Amnesty International works to protect human rights all over the world. We are a movement of ordinary people from across the world, standing up for humanity and human rights. Our purpose is to protect individuals wherever justice, fairness, freedom, and truth are denied.

To find out more about human rights, go to the Student Center at www.amnestyusa.org.

Amnesty International USA, 5 Penn Plaza, New York, NY 10001
(212) 807-8400

Amnesty International

THE ARTICLES OF THE DECLARATION

1 We are all born free and equal. We all have our own thoughts and ideas. We should all be treated in the same way.

2 These rights belong to everybody—whether we are rich or poor, whatever country we live in, whatever sex or whatever color we are, whatever language we speak, whatever we think or whatever we believe.

3 We all have the right to life, and to live in freedom and safety.

4 Nobody has any right to make us a slave. We cannot make anyone else our slave.

5 Nobody has any right to hurt us or to torture us.

6 We all have the same right to be protected by the law.

7 The law is the same for everyone. It must treat us all fairly.

8 We can all ask for the law to help us when we are not treated fairly.

9 Nobody has the right to put us in prison without a good reason, to keep us there, or to send us away from our country.

10 If someone is accused of breaking the law, they have the right to a fair and public trial.

11 Nobody should be blamed for doing something until it has been proved that they did it. If we are accused of a crime, we have the right to defend ourselves. Nobody has the right to condemn us or punish us for something we have not done.

12 Nobody should try to harm our good name. Nobody has the right to come into our home, open our letters, or bother us or our family without a very good reason.

13 We all have the right to go where we want to in our own country and to travel abroad as we wish.

14 If we are frightened of being badly treated in our own country, we all have the right to run away to another country to be safe.

15 We all have the right to belong to a country.

16 Every adult has the right to marry and have a family if they want to. Men and women have the same rights when they are married and when they are separated.

17 Everyone has the right to own things or to share them. Nobody should take our things from us without a good reason.

18 We all have the right to believe in what we want to believe. We have the right to have a religion and to change it if we want.

19 We all have the right to make up our own minds, to think what we like, to say what we think, and to share our ideas with other people, wherever they live, through books, radio, television, and in other ways.

20 We all have the right to meet our friends and to work together in peace to defend our rights. Nobody can make us join a group if we don't want to.

21 We all have the right to take part in the government of our country. Governments should be voted for regularly, and all adults should have the right to a vote. Voting should be secret, and all votes should be equal.

22 We all have the right to a home, to enough money to live on, and to medical help if we are ill. We should all be allowed to enjoy music, art, craft, and sports and to make use of our skills.

23 Every adult has the right to a job, to get a fair wage for their work, and to join a trade union.

24 We all have the right to rest from work and relax.

25 We all have the right to a standard of living that is adequate for our well-being.

26 We all have the right to an education, and to finish elementary school, which should be free. We should be able to learn a career, or to make use of all our skills. We should learn about the United Nations and about how to get along with other people and respect their rights. Our parents have the right to choose how and what we will learn.

27 We all have the right to share in our community's arts and sciences and to enjoy the good things that they bring.

28 We have a right to peace and order so that we can all enjoy rights and freedoms in our own country and all over the world.

29 We have a duty to other people, and we should protect their rights and freedoms.

30 Nobody can take these rights and freedoms from us.

(Simplified version of the Universal Declaration of Human Rights, 1948, by Amnesty International UK; for full text, see www.un.org/en/documents/udhr)